Mum being busy

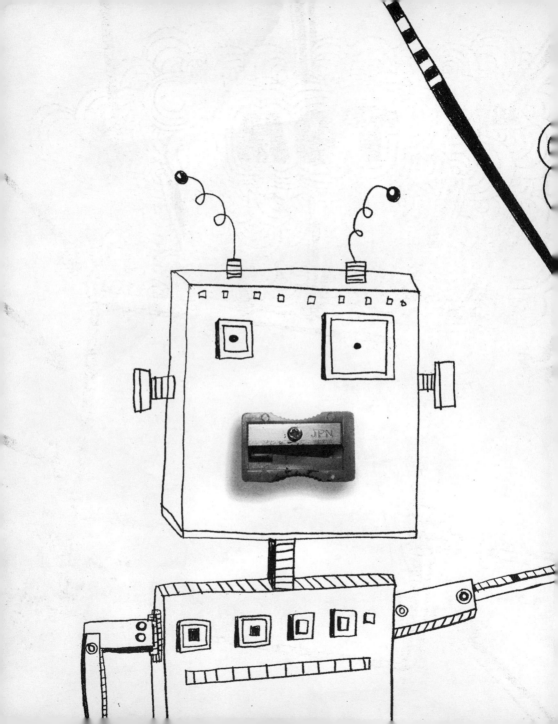

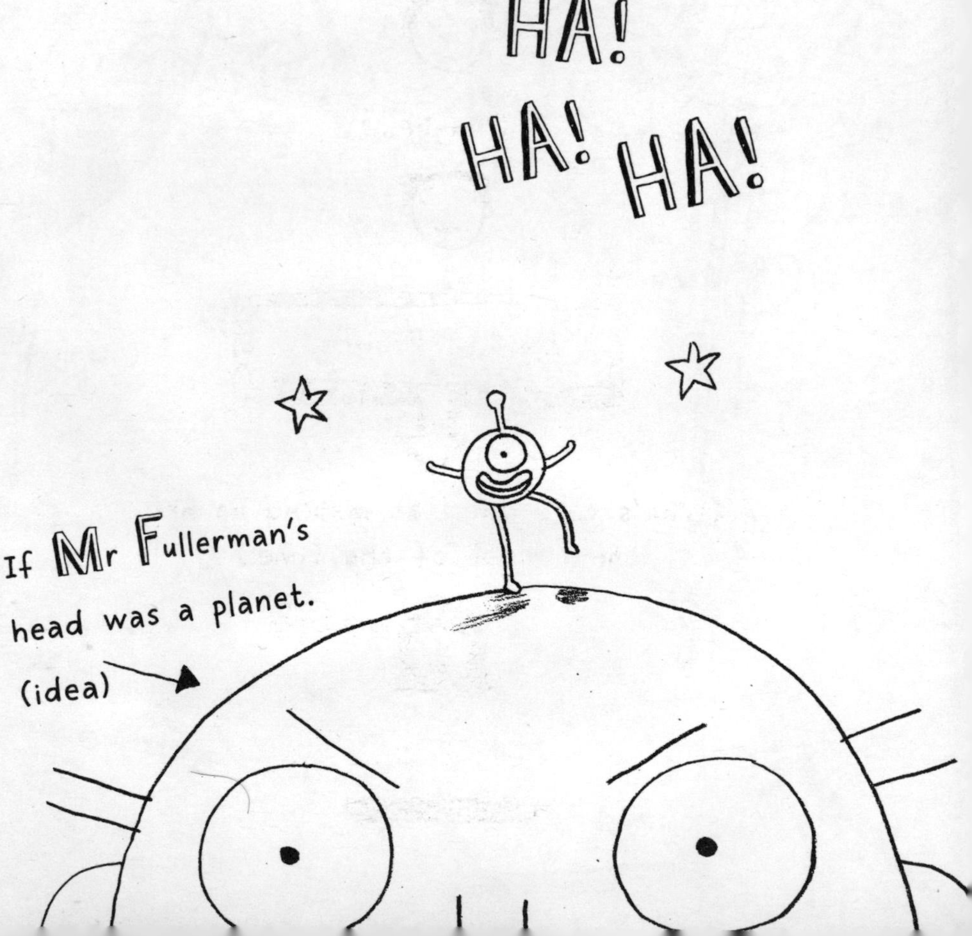
HA!
HA! HA!
If Mr Fullerman's
head was a planet.
(idea)

YES!

NO.

(Maybe...)

By Liz Pichon

(Who's very good at making up her
mind <u>most</u> of the time.)

SCHOLASTIC

Scholastic Children's Books
An imprint of Scholastic Ltd
Euston House, 24 Eversholt Street
London, NW1 1DB, UK

Registered office: Westfield Road,
Southam, Warwickshire, CV47 0RA
SCHOLASTIC and associated logos are trademarks
and/or registered trademarks of Scholastic Inc.

Copyright © Liz Pichon Ltd, 2015
The right of Liz Pichon to be identified
as the author and illustrator
of this work has been asserted by her.

ISBN 978 1407 14879 3

A CIP catalogue record for this book is
available from the British Library

Printed in the UK by CPI Group (UK) Ltd, Croydon, CR0 4YY
Papers used by Scholastic Children's Books are made
from wood grown in sustainable forests.

7 9 10 8

This is a work of fiction. Names, characters,
places, incidents and dialogues are products of the author's imagination
or are used fictitiously. Any resemblance to actual people,
living or dead, events or locales is entirely coincidental.

www.scholastic.co.uk

This 📖 book is dedicated to the lovely Penny Dann♡ who illustrated lots of fabulous books herself. (She liked sausage dogs too.)

Sausage dog

Usually I am very good at making up my mind,  ESPECIALLY when it comes to food.

Mine!

But this morning it's been a bit TRICKY — mostly because Granny Mavis popped round yesterday with a few BITS and PIECES!

INCLUDING a mini SELECTION PACK of breakfast CEREALS, which are my FAVOURITES.

Thanks, Granny!

Coco Loops

Crum

PoP

She brought other stuff as well that didn't look quite so nice. Like TWO packets of SEAWEED -and- WOOD -flavoured CRISPS and a JAR of something ODD that came in Syrup.

? →

SEAWEED & WOOD FLAVOUR CRISPS

Buy One Get One Free!

"I keep forgetting that crisps just get STUCK in your granddad's teeth," Granny told me (like I wanted to know). — Oh.

"So I thought YOU might like them, Tom," she said, passing them to me.

I tried really hard not to pull a "Eeeewww DISGUSTING" kind of face.

Instead I told Granny that she should REALLY give them to Delia.

She LOVES that flavour!

Granny said that I was a "very" thoughtful brother 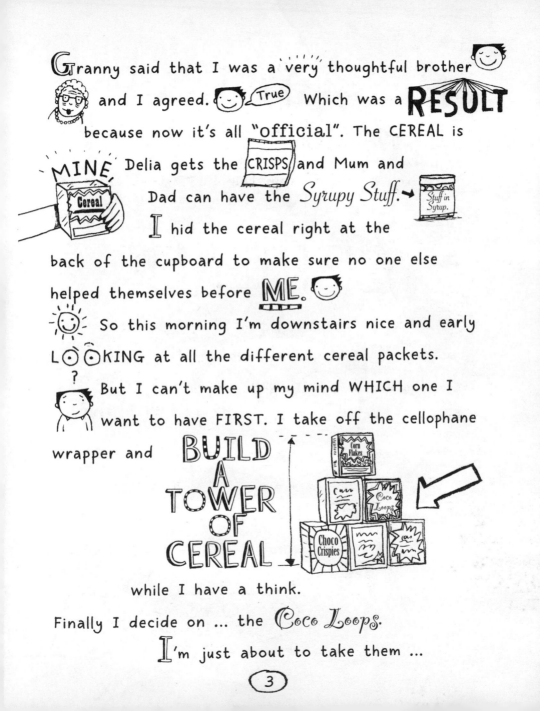 and I agreed. True Which was a **RESULT** because now it's all "official". The CEREAL is MINE Delia gets the CRISPS and Mum and Dad can have the *Syrupy Stuff.* → Stuff in Syrup.

I hid the cereal right at the back of the cupboard to make sure no one else helped themselves before ME.

So this morning I'm downstairs nice and early LOOKING at all the different cereal packets.

But I can't make up my mind WHICH one I want to have FIRST. I take off the cellophane wrapper and BUILD A TOWER OF CEREAL

Corn Flakes
Corn
Coco Loops
Choco Crispies

while I have a think.

Finally I decide on ... the *Coco Loops.*

I'm just about to take them ...

"Don't mind if I do."

"**T**HAT'S **MINE! GIVE IT BACK!**"

I shout.

"**WHO SAYS?**" Delia wants to

know while she opens the cereal.

"Granny bought them for ME. She said I

could have them."

"You have **FIVE** packets left, Tom, I'm

eating this one."

"**NO**, you CAN'T," I say, **PANICKing.**

"**E**rrrr, **YES** I can - WATCH ME."

Delia starts pouring MILK on

to the cereal.

Then she holds the bowl **UP REALLY HIGH**

so I can't reach it.

"This is my breakfast and there's <u>nothing</u> you can

do about it."

Only, she's **WRONG** - there IS something I can do...

≡ I CHARGE around the whole kitchen ≡ and GRAB EVERY single spoon ✑ I can find from EVERYWHERE. (WOODEN SPOONS, tea spoons, BIG SPOONS, the LOT.)

I shove them ALL in a plastic bag and HOLD on to them TIGHTLY.

Delia is watching me. (Is this REALLY happening? she sighs.

There's ONE last spoon right next to the sink ... and we've BOTH seen it.

Delia makes a DASH ≡ BUT I get there FIRST with an EXPERT ≡ floor slide and swipe motion.

"Oh YES, THE SPOON is MINE!" I say as I shove it in the bag.

"Give me that SPOON, Tom."

Delia is getting CROSS.

"Give me my CEREAL," I say. (It's a FAIR swap.)

Then, just to be on the SAFE side, I do another WHIZZ round the kitchen and take all the FORKS as well.

"OK, THAT'S ENOUGH,"

Delia tells me, trying to sound like Mum.

I think she's ready to BARGAIN, so I make a suggestion.

"I'll give you THIS box of PLAIN cornflakes if you give me back my Coco Loops. They're my FAVOURITES."

"They're MY favourites too. Now hand over a spoon."

"**B**ut Granny gave YOU those CRISPS."

(I don't tell her what flavour they are.)

"I don't want CRISPS for breakfast. I want this cereal," Delia says.

I'm GETTING DESPERATE. So I say,

JUST GIVE IT BACK, PLEASE?

Delia starts WALKING towards me.

I'm not EXACTLY sure what she's going to do.

I hold the PLASTIC bag in front of me, then kind of SWING it around a bit to stop her from getting any closer.

Delia can be SNEAKY when she wants something.

"BACK AWAY from the spoons ... and forks," I tell her, in case she gets any ideas.

Delia STOPS, looks down, then very slowly opens a drawer and takes out ...

... SOME CHOPSTICKS?

"You FORGOT about these!" she LAUGHS.

I watch as Delia EXPERTLY picks up the *Coco Loops* one by one with the chopsticks. (I didn't think of THAT.)

There's a **LOUD** clattering sound as I **DROP** the bag with all the spoons and forks. Which INSTANTLY alerts Mum and Dad to something not very good going on downstairs.

CRASH!

"You'll be in trouble **NOW!**" I tell Delia as she carries on eating MY cereal with the chopsticks. She doesn't look that bothered at all. Watching the way Delia is scoffing MY CEREAL, I'm not sure I want it back now.

What WAS that NOISE? And why's that bag on the floor?

Then Dad looks at Delia.

"WHY are you eating with chopsticks?"

"ASK TOM," she says, not looking up.

SO I explain how Granny Mavis gave ME the mini packets of cereal and Delia went and helped herself - sorry - STOLE my favourite packet and is eating them right now.

I took the spoons to try and STOP her... Oh, and the forks too.

Mum says I have to:

1. Put all the cutlery back.

2. Choose another cereal to eat or I'll be late for school.

Then she tells Delia that from NOW ON she should:

1. STOP pinching my cereal. (Better late than never, I suppose.)

2. IN future be a LOT more MATURE (which makes her sound like an old piece of cheese).

(Cheese ss pong)

Ha! Ha!

"If it will STOP you two arguing, I'll BUY another [P][A][C][K] of mini cereal," Mum tells us in a slightly irritated voice.

←Delia   Tom→

I nod ("   ") and Delia mumbles something in-between mouthfuls.

BUT then Mum goes and ADDS,

Sometime soon.   Which is a WORRY

because whenever she says   Sometime soon.

It usually means   NOT VERY SOON AT ALL.

OR   Probably NEVER.

Mum tells me AGAIN,   I promise I'll buy more, Tom.

(I'm not convinced.)

If ONLY I hadn't taken SO long to make up my mind, NONE of this would have happened. (-_-)

I take my SECOND-favourite choice (Choco Crispies) and put them in a bowl before THEY get taken too.

"EAT UP or you'll be late for school!" Mum tells me.

I point out I've only got FOUR packets left now.

Make that three packets, Tom — we've run out of my muesli,

Mum says while helping herself to the cornflakes (which I'm not bothered about).

BUT THESE are MINE.

I slip the LAST packets into my school bag for safe keeping and I'm about to leave when Mum SHOUTS,

TOM! Aren't you forgetting something?

(Uh-oh!)

Go and brush your teeth, will you?

(Phew!)

I hope she hasn't spotted the cereal in my bag.

I brush my teeth, and when I come back
Mum doesn't mention anything. She's busy
chatting to Dad and discussing what we're
doing this weekend.

"NOTHING. Why, what's happening?"
Dad says, looking confused.

We're not doing ANYTHING?

Nope

OK, we have nothing planned for this
weekend OR next weekend either?

Mum asks AGAIN. I get ready to leave when she
adds,

Have a great
day, Tom.

But not in a JOLLY way.   I'll try.

As I walk out of the door, Delia "RUFFLES" my
hair with her hand.

"Thanks for breakfast, little brother.
Remember, it's GOOD to share," she says.
But I'm not sure she means it.

"What's up with your hair?" Derek asks me.

"That was Delia. She's been annoying me ALL morning." I tell Derek how she NICKED my cereal.

"I've brought the rest of them with me in case she takes THOSE as well. I might just HIDE everything in my room from now on."

"You're lucky. Anything I hide, Rooster finds then eats," Derek says.

(Which is true, I've seen him.)

My room's a bit messy at the moment, so hiding things is EASY. The tricky bit's finding them again.

Before

Where's my water?

After

15

Derek and I are doing *FAST* walking to school to make sure we're not late, when he says,

> I've got something to tell you about June's dad.

(June is the slightly annoying girl who lives next door to me and goes to our school, and her dad used to be in a BAND called **PLASTIC CUP**.)

I ask, "What about June's dad?" But Derek starts **COUGHING** and can't get it out.

COUGH COUGH

> June's dad? I say again,

when Derek STOPS coughing.

"You know how **MY** dad won't stop going on about June's dad being in **PLASTIC CUP?**"

> SLIGHTLY. He's a BIG fan, I say.

Derek's dad

PLASTIC CUP

I'm a FAN!

Derek agrees then does an impression of HIS dad.

"He keeps on saying, 'They should get back together and make a NEW record.'"

I remind Derek, "That **PLASTIC CUP** album we listened to the other day was 'GREAT!'"

(IT'S TRUE. I was SURPRISED.)

"Well, you'll never guess what my dad did." I'm CURIOUS now. WHAT?

"He went over to JUNE'S HOUSE wearing a **PLASTIC CUP** T-SHIRT and told him he had to make a **NEW RECORD!**"

— New record

Huh?

SHAME.

"And I found out something else..."

What?

"My dad says that the **PLASTIC CUP** album we were listening to is WORTH **LOADS** of MONEY."

Really?

"BUT only if it's not scratched OR broken."

Oh...   I say, for good reason ...

... because I've just remembered what we

did at our last band practice.

(Whoops.)

I sit down at my desk next to Marcus Meldrew, who immediately *LEANS* away from me.

The first thing he says is,

You haven't got the **BUG**, have you, Tom?

"What bug?"

"There's a lot of kids coughing and off SICK and I don't want to catch anything because it's an IMPORTANT week for me."

"Why's that?"

Marcus starts ROLLING his eyes like I've asked a really stupid question.

"Don't you remember ANYTHING, Tom?"

Then Amy Porter sits down on the other side of me and she says, "It's the school's **Business DAY** coming up and we're supposed to be thinking up IDEAS."

I knew that. (I didn't.)

"I've got a BRILLIANT idea and whatever group I'm in will raise the most money for sure." Marcus sounds very positive and KEEN, which makes me wonder what his BRILLIANT idea is.

So I ask him.

"Nice try, Tom. I'm not telling you anything. You might PINCH my idea."

"I have my OWN ideas, Marcus. I don't need yours," I say.

We'll SEE... Marcus says.

← Smug

Every year the kids in our school raise money for charity by selling things they've made. Some stuff is more POPULAR than others.

(Toilet rolls)

Pen holders

Yeah!

Marshmallow & Fruit Kebabs

?

I ♡ School
I ♡ School
I ♡ School

Badges

We're not allowed to sell  SWEETS or FIZZY DRINKS

BUT ... home-made CAKES are always popular.

Especially with **ME!**

Mr Fullerman is sitting at his desk now and says,

"SETTLE DOWN, Class 5F."

COUGH! Then he starts **COUGHING!**
COUGH!
COUGH!

The first thing I notice is that Mr Fullerman is

NOT looking like his normal self.

He looks a bit ... **GREY**.

"GOOD MORNING, EVERYONE."

"Good morning, Mr Fullerman," we

say back.

Mr Fullerman isn't the only one coughing.

I turn round to see who it is.

COUGH!
COUGH!

Quite a few kids are _MISSING_ but Norman's there so I 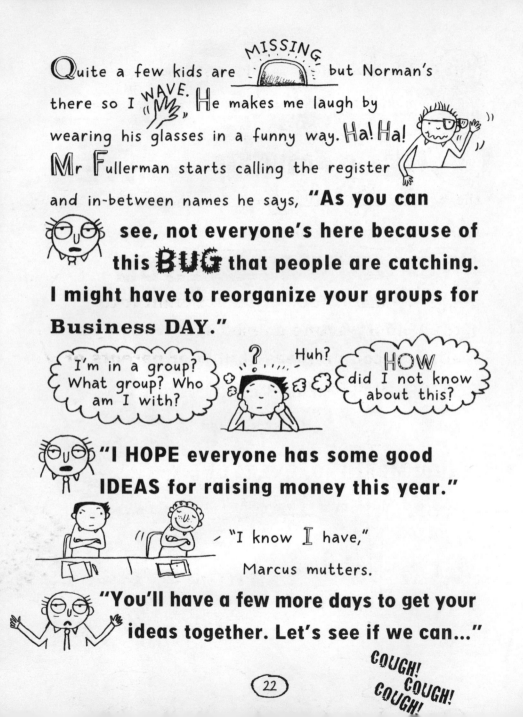 "WAVE." He makes me laugh by wearing his glasses in a funny way. Ha! Ha! Mr Fullerman starts calling the register and in-between names he says, **"As you can see, not everyone's here because of this BUG that people are catching. I might have to reorganize your groups for Business DAY."**

I'm in a group? What group? Who am I with?

? ... Huh?

HOW did I not know about this?

"I HOPE everyone has some good IDEAS for raising money this year."

"I know I have," Marcus mutters.

"You'll have a few more days to get your ideas together. Let's see if we can..."

COUGH! COUGH! COUGH!

Mr Fullerman CLASPS his hand over his mouth to STOP coughing. He's saved when the bell goes off for assembly.

There's more COUGHING going on in the hall too. Mr Keen (our headmaster) is standing in front of everyone and says,

There seems to be a bit of a BUG going around school. We don't want it to spread, so if anyone doesn't feel well or has a really bad cough, please tell your parents or carers to keep you off school.

As SOON as Mr Keen says the words ...

"KEEP YOU OFF SCHOOL"

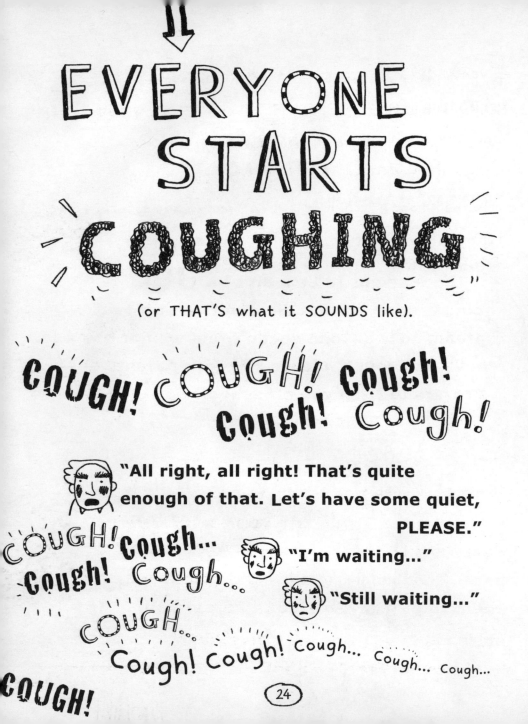

EVERYONE STARTS COUGHING

(or THAT'S what it SOUNDS like).

COUGH! COUGH! Cough! Cough! Cough!

"All right, all right! That's quite enough of that. Let's have some quiet, PLEASE."

COUGH! Cough... Cough! Cough...

"I'm waiting..."

COUGH... "Still waiting..."

Cough! Cough! Cough... Cough... Cough...

COUGH!

24

Eventually the coughing dies down and Mr Keen begins talking again. Even though I feel absolutely fine and don't have a **BUG** or a `cough,` being surrounded by kids who are **coughing** makes me want to **cough!** My throat's gone a bit dry and TICKLY.

As soon as Mr Keen starts talking again, the TICKLE gets a LOT WORSE.

I'm trying to STOP myself from **coughing.**

Mr Fullerman is STARING at me because I'm fidgeting a lot now.

shhh

COUGH! COUGH! COUGH!

Then Marcus nudges me and says, "Shhhhhhhh."

Somehow I keep it under control while Mr Keen announces that **"There are some very clever Year Three children who have won a poetry prize. They're going to read out their winning poem right now. So LISTEN carefully, no more coughing, and let's give them a big round of APPLAUSE!"**

At this point my THROAT goes CRAZY.
The loud "CLAPPING" noise covers me while I try
and clear my throat.

COUGH!
Cough!
COUGH!
Cough...

The WHOLE school is REALLY quiet as the kids begin
to read their poem (with movement and sound effects).

You could hear a PIN

DROP.

"Branches bend and CREAK slowly."
CREAKKK

"The BOY stares UP at the COLD
blue sky and SIGHS."

SIGHHH

26

"Then watches the LEAVES SWAY..."

Whoosh Whoosh

"...as the WIND WHISTLES..."

Whistle Whistle

"...the birds TWITTER..."

Twitter Twitter

"...and then the BOY BEGINS TO..."

COUGH! Cough! Cough... Cough! COUGH... Cough! Cough! Cough! Cough! Cough! Cough!

(That bit's not in the poem - but I just can't help myself.)

The kids around me have LURCHED away so the teachers can see who's making all the NOISE.

EVERYONE is staring at me.

Mr Keen doesn't look happy at all. Mr Fullerman waves at me FURIOUSLY to get up and leave the hall. Quickly! **"Have a drink of water, Tom,"** he croaks as I stagger past him **coughing** all the way.

The GOOD NEWS IS, the water does the trick and I'm FINE now. 😊 It's a very long poem that seems to go on for AGES. So I take the opportunity to LOOK at the school noticeboard.

There's stuff on there about the school's **Business DAY.** And Mr Fullerman's picture is RIGHT next to the news of a school TRIP to the ZOO. Ha! Ha!

Mr Fullerman's eyes look like the lemur's!

OAKFIELD SCHOOL NOTICEBOARD

Mr Fullerman

THIS WEEK it's Mr Fullerman's turn to recommend a favourite book. He's chosen JUST WILLIAM by Richmal Crompton, which was written a long time ago about a schoolboy called William.

"I think a lot of my class would enjoy the kinds of things William got up to. But I'm not encouraging them to behave like him!"

You can get JUST WILLIAM from the library. Or ask Miss Pencil for other recommendations. There are LOADS of great books to choose from.

LOST PROPERTY

FIND YOUR STUFF

Ha! Ha!

Are these yours?

YEAR FOUR VISIT TO THE ZOO

Year Four had a fantastic trip to the zoo. They were taken on a tour and shown all kinds of interesting animals.

There is an exhibition of their wonderful work in the hall.

We particularly liked the ring-tailed lemurs with the VERY BIG EYES.

DON'T FORGET IT'S SCHOOL Business DAY! There'll be LOTS to BUY.

The WINNER of the POETRY competition

I'm still laughing at the picture when my class comes out of the hall. I show it to Solid and Norman, who think it's funny too.

Back at my desk, Marcus says,

> I thought you weren't SICK?

"I'm NOT. I just had a tickly throat."

"Well, just in case, I'm going to STAY OUT of your way."

Which suits me FINE.

As Mr Fullerman begins the lesson there's a spare piece of paper on my desk which REALLY needs a drawing on it.

LIKe THiS...

(I've been inspired by all kinds of things.)

While I'm drawing 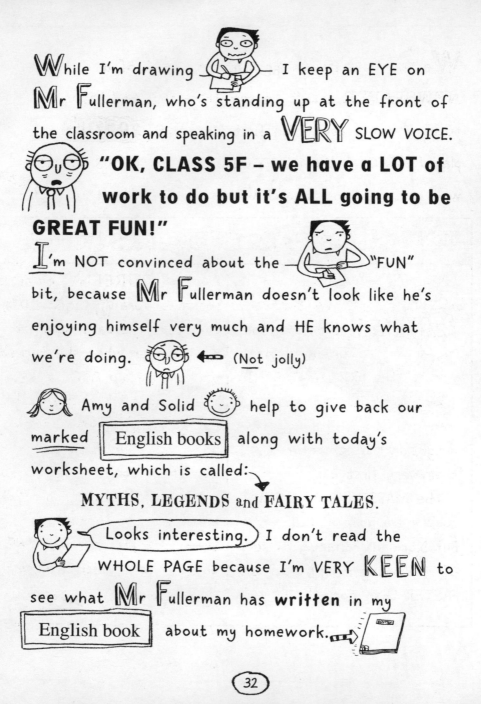 I keep an EYE on **M**r **F**ullerman, who's standing up at the front of the classroom and speaking in a **VERY** SLOW VOICE.

"OK, CLASS 5F – we have a LOT of work to do but it's ALL going to be GREAT FUN!"

I'm NOT convinced about the "FUN" bit, because **M**r **F**ullerman doesn't look like he's enjoying himself very much and HE knows what we're doing. ⟵ (<u>Not</u> jolly)

Amy and Solid help to give back our <u>marked</u> | English books | along with today's worksheet, which is called:

MYTHS, LEGENDS and **FAIRY TALES.**

(Looks interesting.) I don't read the WHOLE PAGE because I'm VERY **KEEN** to see what **M**r **F**ullerman has **written** in my | English book | about my homework.

We had to write a report in the STYLE of a NEWSPAPER article on something that had happened to us. I wrote about the first time **DOGZOMBIES** played a **GIG** at the LEAFY GREEN OLD FOLK'S HOME, which was a good idea. I wrote stuff like this:

TOP BAND ROCKS OLD FOLK'S HOME

Norman Watson (aged 9), the drummer in the BRILLIANT BAND **DOGZOMBIES**, somehow managed to EAT his body weight in biscuits before their very first gig.

The MASSIVE sugar rush could have been a disaster. But Norman managed to keep ON drumming – only he went FASTER than normal.

LEAFY GREEN'S oldest resident, Vera (aged 101), said that the band sounded much better when she turned her hearing aid OFF.

"It was a bit loud for me. But **DOGZOMBIES** are lovely boys and their music has a good beat to it."

Most of the other old folk enjoyed a good singalong though. It was a sell-out gig and the band celebrated with caramel wafers and squash.

I was REALLY pleased :) with my REPORT and I'm HOPING for GREAT comments from Mr Fullerman like:

Well done, TOM, a SUPERB and BRILLIANT piece of reporting. TEN MERITS.

OR

FANTASTIC WORK, TOM! Take the REST of the week off and give yourself a BIG TREAT! TEN MERITS.

Not THIS!

Tom, you seem to be missing a piece of work here. Where's your report?

WHAT? NO!

I spent AGES on that piece of homework. (I really did.) There's nothing more annoying than DOING some GOOD WORK on TIME, but still getting ⟶ NO MERITS.

Where's it gone? Maybe I dropped it in my room. OR Delia's hidden it because I borrowed her **ROCK WEEKLY.**

Ha Ha!

I really hope Rooster hasn't eaten it.

(That's happened to Derek before.)

Oh no, Rooster!

I'll have a good SEARCH when I get home. I won't mention the "missing homework" to Mum, because she'll just say,

It's probably in your MESSY bedroom. That's why you need to tidy UP!

SIGH...

Marcus keeps shoving his book under my nose.

"**S**EE! I got **TWO** MERITS.

What did you get?"

"I got TONS of merits and good comments. My report is **SO** AMAZING I'm actually embarrassed to show you," I say convincingly.

Then I turn over to a FRESH page so he can't see the "MISSING WORK" comment. Marcus is <u>still</u> being a NOSY PARKER while **M**r **F**ullerman tells us about the TOPIC for TODAY.

I'm listening, but **M**r **F**ullerman's VOICE is getting harder to understand.

 So I find myself drawing ...

Ag**A**i**N**.

I start in this corner...

Then I do a bit more here ➔

My doodle starts to

GROW BIGGER

I write my name, TOM, then I think about LUNCH.  Who might be in my **business group**? Then lunch again. Marcus is STILL watching me and he *NUDGES* my arm, which makes me joq

"Tom, why have you written Amy's name in your BOOK?" he wants to know.

"What? I HAVEN'T written Amy's name."

"Yes, you have ... SEE."

He points at my book.

"THAt's NOt..."

(Oh ... it is. I have.)

A
M
Y

"I TOLD you. Why are you writing her name, Tom?" (I was thinking about WHO might be in my **business group**, that's ALL.)

But I don't SAY that because luckily I have a BRAINWAVE and I WHISPER, "Ssshhh... I don't want Mr Fullerman to hear. It might LOOK like I've written "AMY" but I'm just about to turn it into a MONSTER."

Marcus says, "Yeah, RIGHT," like he doesn't believe me.

So I say, "Watch this, I'll show you how to turn AMY (the word) into a MONSTER."

Then Amy turns round and says,

"Did you just call me a monster?"

NO, not you!

(This isn't working out at ALL.)

I turn my book round then make her name into a
WEIRD-looking creature while Amy watches.

Like this

"That's actually quite funny,"
Amy says, looking at my drawing
and trying not to laugh.

Which makes ME laugh...
(But not for long.)

Mr Fullerman CROAKS at us.
"Concentrate ... both of you."

Cough...

I INSTANTLY put down my pencil and start STUDYING my worksheet. "Yes, sir."

AMY is concentrating on hers too.

As soon as he's gone I pick up my pencil and do another NAME doodle.

THIS is more  *FUN* than I thought!

Whose name shall I do NEXT that will make a good MONSTER?

Hmmmmmm? Let me see.

It's obvious, really.

Hmmmm

What?

MARCUS

Draw the letters like this (mirrored shapes)

Then add the FUN bits!

HA!
Ha! HA!

Today is turning out to be quite a GOOD day after all. As part of ART, we've been given THIS BRILLIANT **SKETCHBOOK!**

There's a worksheet too, explaining what we're supposed to be DRAWING in it for this project.

So I take a look...

SKETCHBOOK

ART TOPIC for CLASS 5F

EXPRESSIONS
FACES OF PEOPLE AND ANIMALS

This term we're going to be looking at facial expressions. So using your pens, pencils and paints, I'd like you to fill your sketchbook up with as many different types of FACIAL EXPRESSION as you can.

You can do self-portraits by looking at yourself in the mirror and sketching what you see. But better still, draw from real life, and the things you see around you.

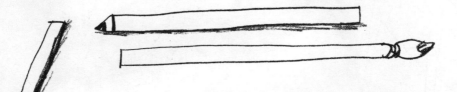

Draw people or animals to show a wide variety of different expressions, and have FUN!

I take back what I said about TODAY being a GOOD day because my lunchtime was RUBBISH. Lots of things went wrong.

STARTING WITH:

1. Me joining the WRONG queue for lunch. (I only found out when I got to the front.)

Rumble, rumble

Sign up for the homework club?

Lunch →

2. Then I joined the RIGHT queue but missed out on all the GOOD FOOD.

3. I had to choose between NASTY GREY mince OR vegetable bake.

Peas

Chips GOnE

NASTY GREY MinCE

Vegetable BAKE

I had the vegetable bake ...

4. ... which wasn't that nice and tasted more like vegetable MUSH.

5. AND because I didn't finish it, I wasn't allowed SECONDS OF PUDDING, which was HARSH.

6. Then to TOP it all, the little kids beat me at CHAMP - AGAIN. (I was trying really hard too.)

miss

Huh!

Loser!

Champ

1
2
3

So I'm back in my class wondering why I'm having SUCH a BAD day, when I notice someone else is sitting at Mr Fullerman's desk.

IT'S ONLY MRS MUMBLE,

(who's a lot smaller than Mr Fullerman). - - - - - - - - ▶

Mrs Mumble

Hello, Class 5F. I'm VERY sorry to tell you that Mr Fullerman had to go home because he's not feeling very well. -Cough! Cough!

Somebody says, "YES!" just a little bit too LOUDLY. (Brad Galloway.)

He's looking over his shoulder pretending it wasn't him. Which MIGHT have worked if Julia Morton had actually been sitting there. (She's off sick too.) EMPTY CHAIR

Mrs Mumble puts on her CROSS VOICE.

Anything else to say, BRAD?

"No, Mrs Mumble."

I'll carry on then. Until Mr Fullerman feels better someone **VERY** important will be covering your lessons today. **Aren't you LUCKY?**

(Hmmmm... That sort of depends on who it is.)

Mrs Mumble holds up the worksheet on

Mr Fullerman's desk.

"**MYTHS, LEGENDS** and **FAIRY TALES**. What an interesting topic. I L♡VE fairy tales. Does anyone here have a favourite?"

Amber puts her hand up.

"Who's teaching us today, Mrs Mumble?" Which isn't exactly what she was asking for.

"Well, you'll see now, because here they are..." The door starts to open and we're all STARING ➡ when in walks ...

Mr Keen - our HEADMASTER.

"Hello, Class 5F. I'm just as **SURPRISED** as you are that I'm here!"

(Errrrr... I don't think so.) Huh?

Then Mrs Mumble says,

"This LOVELY class are ready to work very **HARD** for you, Mr Keen."

(S I L E N C E .)

He's holding a **MASSIVE** pile of paper that I don't like the look of either. I have a horrible feeling that the paper is **EXTRA** homework for us. And we'll end up getting detention if it's not **ALL** done.

This lesson hasn't even STARTED yet and I'm NOT enjoying it already.

Mr Keen begins by telling us, **"You'll be PLEASED to hear that Mr Fullerman has left me some work for you to do while he's away."**

(Me not being pleased)

Groan

I groan a bit – but nothing too loud, as I don't want to get into trouble.

 "LET'S GET STARTED, SHALL WE?"

Mr Keen adds happily.

 I have a TERRIBLE feeling that this is going to be the WORST lesson in the WHOLE WIDE WORLD.

EVERY minute will feel like an hour. creak

Then every HOUR will feel like a WHOLE YEAR. (OK, maybe just a DAY – but it will still take AGES.)

Mr Keen will make this lesson really DULL and boring. I just know it. Blah Blah Blah Blah

(If things get too dull I might have to start COUGHING again.) SIGH!

Cough... Cough...

I turn over to a NICE plain page and get ready to do some doodling. Which will keep me occupied during Mr Keen's L O N G boring lesson.

(Pens at the ready)

It will also |look| like I'm taking NOTES
and concentrating, so hopefully I won't get
into trouble.

Here goes. Yawn...

YEAH!

WHAT A SURPRISE!

THAT lesson was one of the MOST **FUN** lessons EVER! It was super good because all we had to do was watch a FILM about **Robin Hood** (not the cartoon version - but you can't have everything). And the pile of paper Mr Keen had wasn't for us after all. It was LOADS of his <u>own</u> work.

I learnt all kinds of good things about **Robin Hood** (who was a LEGEND). STUFF LIKE:

Fancy hat

Cash

Green

* He wore mostly GREEN CLOTHES and a fancy hat with a feather.
* He was handy with a bow and arrow.
* He lived in a forest ... and stole money from the rich to give to the poor.

* His friends were called MERRY MEN
(even though some of them weren't
"merry" at all).

(Not very merry)

Who knew that Mr Keen would make our MYTHS,
LEGENDS and FAIRY TALES lesson SO GOOD?

(Not me, that's for sure.)

Mind you, there was ONE little problem with the
lesson. Mr Keen decided to move his desk so
EVERYONE in the class could see the TV screen better.
EVERYONE, that was, APART from ME.

(Mr Keen's HEAD
in the way) →

I didn't want to make a FUSS in case he *pushed*
his desk even CLOSER to mine. So I decided to use
my school BAG like a CUSHION and sit on it so I
could SEE over his head.

It was a GOOD plan.

Bag
→

But for some reason my bag wasn't exactly comfortable. I had to WRIGGLE around a LOT  to get settled. It felt like I was sitting on a couple of BOOKS. So I jumped up and down, which seemed to help.

Squish

That's better

It was only when I came home from school that I remembered what I'd put inside my bag to keep SAFE.

Oh ..., wasn't books then

There's squashed CEREAL everywhere, which explains the crunching sound Derek could hear on the way home.

Crunch

What's that crunchy noise?

STARING at the cereal now is making me hungry, so I take a look round the kitchen for something ELSE I can eat that's not so SQUISHED.

And I can't BELIEVE it when I spot ANOTHER packet of mini CEREAL that Mum must have bought.

Which is a BIG surprise.

I help myself to a NEW box of Coco Loops without Delia pinching it this time and eat it up pretty FAST. YUM!

It's all gone... (Unlike the cereal in my bag, which is still there.)

I deal with the slightly crunchy MESS by tipping everything on to the table.

Then I use my hand to SCRAPE the cereal BACK into the empty box. This way Mum won't suspect I've already eaten a packet as it still looks like NEW.

I am a GENIUS! (True)

Being a GENIUS doesn't help me find my pyjamas that evening, though. They turn up eventually ...

Messy bedroom →

Comics →

Stuff △ everywhere

Result

... under my bed, along with a BIG stack of comics I'd forgotten about AND a half-eaten caramel wafer

– which is a RESULT!

I'm LUCKY to have a bedroom all to myself. Some of my friends have to share with a brother or sister (like Norman Watson does).

Mark Clump keeps loads of pets and creatures in his room. I'd LOVE a pet but Delia is ALLERGIC to most ANIMALS, so I don't suppose that's EVER going to happen.

If she's around CATS or DOGS for too long, she starts SNEEZING, Go Away which makes her even grumpier.

The same thing happens to me if I'm around Delia for too long. (Not the sneezing bit – the being grumpy.)

I've asked Mum and Dad LOADS of times if I could get a pet and they ALWAYS say the same thing.

Sorry, Tom, we can't have pets in the house because of Delia.

They suggest I get a FISH. But watching a fish swim up and down isn't very exciting. Not unless I had more than ONE.

Then I would **TRAIN** them all to do tricks  and have races.

Which would be **ACE.**

So far the closest I've ever got to having my own **PET** is taking Rooster out for walks with Derek.

Sometimes we play games in his garden too.

Derek's been **TRYING** to teach Rooster a few **TRICKS.**

By now he's learnt to:

Roll over

SIT

Play dead

JUMP!

DANCE

DANCE!...

(We're still working on that one.)

I'd ALWAYS be in a good mood if

I had a dog that could DANCE.

June (who lives on the other side of me) has

got a cat called Roger. He's a LOT friendlier

now than he used to be - which isn't that hard.

(June is about the same.)

The other day Roger came into our garden

and wanted me to stroke him, which hasn't

happened before. Mum spotted him through the

kitchen window and went CRAZY! She

rushed out waving her arms around and

SHOUTING, **SHOO! SHOO!**

until Roger jumped back over the fence.

"Don't encourage that CAT to come in our garden, Tom," Mum told me. Then she pointed at some green stalks with NO flowers. "He's been chewing and RUINING all my plants. LOOK at my flower bed!"

Mum wasn't happy at all. "That CAT," she said, pointing at Roger this time, "must have SNEAKED into our garden and EATEN all the tops off the flowers! He's a FURRY MENACE!" Mum said angrily.

Roger can be a nuisance sometimes.

Yowwwwwl
Yowwwwwl

—But he didn't eat the flowers, because I know what REALLY happened.

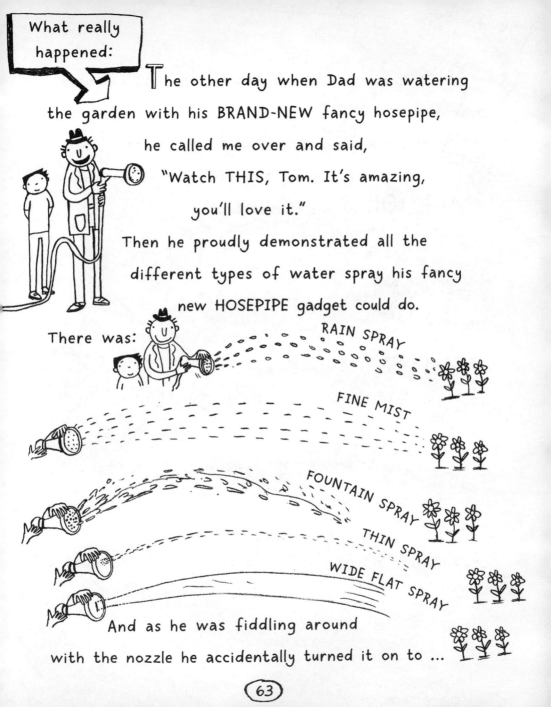

What really happened:

The other day when Dad was watering the garden with his BRAND-NEW fancy hosepipe, he called me over and said,

"Watch THIS, Tom. It's amazing, you'll love it."

Then he proudly demonstrated all the different types of water spray his fancy new HOSEPIPE gadget could do.

There was:

RAIN SPRAY

FINE MIST

FOUNTAIN SPRAY

THIN SPRAY

WIDE FLAT SPRAY

And as he was fiddling around with the nozzle he accidentally turned it on to ...

TURBO-JET-POWERED SPRAY

THE WATER SHOT OUT OF THE HOSE ALL SO FAST THAT IT BLASTED THE PETALS OFF THE FLOWERS, AND SOME OF THEIR HEADS SNAPPED OFF TOO.

It only took a few seconds and the whole flower bed WAS RUINED.

Dad PANICKED and let go of the hosepipe, which started to wriggle around, spraying water everywhere. He was wrestling the hose like it was a GIANT SNAKE and SHOUTING at me to,

"TURN OFF the TAP, TOM - QUICKLY!"

Ha! Ha!

I was laughing SO much I couldn't work out which way was OFF.

"WRONG WAY! WRONG WAY!"

Dad shouted, so I turned the tap in the other direction. When it FINALLY stopped spraying, Dad looked a bit damp and his feet were soaking wet too.

But the flower bed looked worse.

"I'll have to get some more flowers. Don't mention this to your mother," Dad told me and sighed.

When Mum saw the state of the garden, she blamed the CAT  STRAIGHT AWAY.

LOOK WHAT THAT CAT'S done to the FLOWERS – it's chewed them ALL UP!

Dad kept quiet and so did I. He was happy for the CAT to take the blame.

But now those flowers have become ANOTHER REASON I'm not allowed to get a PET. Sigh...

IF I could get a pet it would probably be a DOG. Nothing HUGE or with  LONG FUR that needed loads of washing and brushing. I'd solve the problem of Delia being allergic to pets by making her wear a

SPACESUIT all the time.

Which isn't a bad idea anyway.

Brilliant!

(One giant grumpy step)

Another thing I'd do if I had a dog is TRAIN it to find things for me. SO useful! Imagine being able to say, "Go find my sock!"

Or even, **Where's my HOMEWORK?**

My dog would have found my REPORT HOMEWORK

yesterday, no problem.

I have been TRYING to find my report homework. But sometimes when you're looking for one thing – you find something else.

Like this comic folder* I made AGES ago.

I was wondering where it had gone to.

(I got the idea from a book Mum bought me called **DON'T GET BORED, GET BUSY!**)

I'd forgotten how good they look too. ☺

Me looking under my bed

* See page 258 on how to make a comic folder.

This one's the right size for my sketchbook. I pop them both in my bag so I don't forget to bring them to school with me.

(There's still some cereal lurking inside my bag — which I ignore.)

I'm all set for tomorrow now. Excellent.

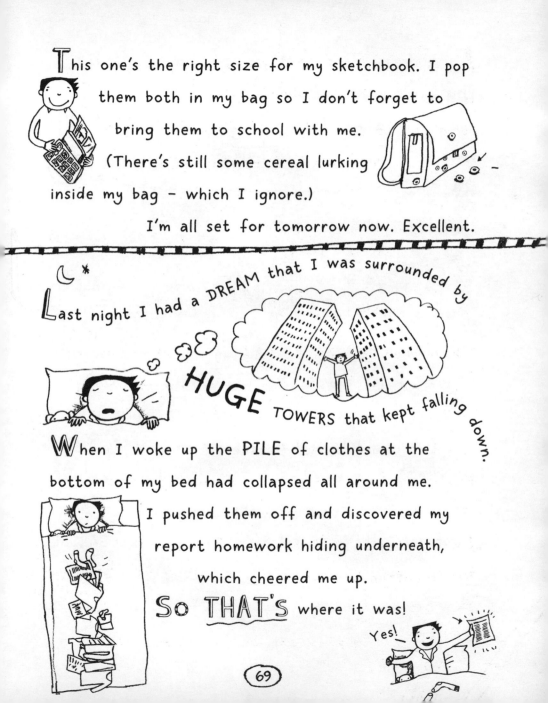

Last night I had a DREAM that I was surrounded by HUGE TOWERS that kept falling down.

When I woke up the PILE of clothes at the bottom of my bed had collapsed all around me.

I pushed them off and discovered my report homework hiding underneath, which cheered me up.

So THAT'S where it was!

Yes!

I get dressed and go downstairs where Mum's "chatting" with Dad about various different things, like what's happening over the next TWO weekends. Dad says, "Nothing special unless we get a SURPRISE visit from Kevin and Alice, but we could always pretend to be OUT." (We've done that before.)

Mum says, "We're doing a boot sale THIS WEEKEND, OK?" When Dad hears the words boot sale he immediately starts trying to think of reasons he's BUSY. "Oh, hang on ... maybe we have got something on after all. I think Tom's got an important ... SPORTS practice or BAND REHEARSAL and he needs my help. Don't you, Tom?"

(Which is news to me.) So I say ...

"No, I haven't."

Dad GLARES at me like I've said the wrong thing. (Dad is right, though. **DOGZOMBIES** does need to practise more.)

Mum tells us, "That's settled, then – we'll do a BIG house clear-out for a boot sale this weekend. Then we can save the weekend AFTER for doing something else."

"That's great," Dad says (but not in a happy way).

It's only after Mum's gone to work that Dad realizes why Mum KEEPS asking what we're doing at the weekends.

 "OF COURSE! It's your mum's BIRTHDAY!"

"Did you forget?" I ask him, because it sounds like he did.

"Of course I didn't forget," Dad tells me. (Dad forgot.) Ha! Ha!

To be fair, I hadn't remembered either.

"What are you going to get Mum for her birthday?" I ask Dad.

"I have **NO** idea," Dad says, sounding a bit desperate. So I do my best to be helpful.

"There is SOMETHING Mum would LOVE."

"What's that, TOM?"

"I think she'd be SO HAPPY if you got her ..."

"YES?"

"... the BEST present EVER."

"Which is?"

"A PUPPY."

Woof!

"Nice try, Tom."

(Oh well, it was worth a go.)

Here are a few drawings of dogs in my sketchbook.

SKETCHBOOK

TOM Gates

EXPRESSIONS

Self-portrait of ME if I had a DOG

HAPPY FACE

Different dogs that could be my pet

Delia if I got a pet

Ha! Ha! Ha!

Roger (June's cat) if I → got a dog

SCHOOL STUFF

I've brought my COMIC folder with my sketchbook inside to school. I might have the chance to use it in class if I'm lucky.

Mr Keen has gone back to being a headmaster, which is a shame because I liked watching FILMS in lessons. INSTEAD we've had ALL these teachers.

Mrs Worthington ⟹

Hello, Tom!

Groan

Mrs Mumble

No doodling, Tom!

Groan

⟸ Mr Sprocket

Shame

And NOW we've got Miss Yodel, who's not been at our school very long. She's supposed to be "FUNNY", but not in the way you might think.

HELLO, CLASS 5F. I'M MISS YODEL

YooODDDELLLYYYYYYY!

(Miss Yodel ... yodels.)

The first time she does it in our class, it takes everyone by surprise. **AMY** tells me,

I heard she does that a lot.

Miss Yodel is writing on the board while reminding us about how <u>close</u> **Business DAY** is.

"IT'S COMING UP VERY SOON, WHICH IS EXCITING... YoddeLLEEEY!"

(It's such a weird sound.)

Then she lets us know what groups we are in and does ANOTHER YODEL.

YooODDDELLLYYYYYYY!

Solid put up his hand and says,

"Are you OK, Miss Yodel?" Which makes me laugh.

Ha! Ha! Ha! (I'm not the only one.) But LAUGHING at Solid has made me forget WHAT **business group** I'm in.

Luckily, Miss Yodel sticks a list up.

So I take a sneaky L⊙⊙K.

I'm with **AMY**, LEROY, PANSY, SOLID and ... Marcus. Oh, great.

(Let's hope he's not too annoying.)

"SIT DOWN, TOM," Miss Yodel says (not yodelling). Then she adds, "RIGHT, CLASS, I'D LIKE YOU TO GET INTO YOUR GROUPS AND CHAT THROUGH ALL YOUR **business ideas**. WRITE THEM DOWN SO YOU CAN TELL THE REST OF THE CLASS WHAT YOU'LL BE DOING."

Which sounds easy enough – unless Marcus Meldrew is in your group. It doesn't take long for him to take over.

Me first...

Here we go

"I have the BEST idea. It's always popular and we should do this before anyone else does."

"What's your idea, Marcus?" I ask.

FACE-PAINTING, EVERYONE LOVES IT!

It's not a **terrible** idea.

"But Only the little kids will want their faces painted," Pansy tells him.

"And I'm not very good at face-painting," Leroy adds.

"It's EASY. You use STENCILS with a sponge and it's a LOT quicker too. Trust me – EVERYONE LOVES FACE-PAINTING!"

"Not EVERYONE – I don't," AMY says.

"Good POINT," I agree with AMY, and Marcus gives me a look.

"I'm telling you, kids LOVE FACE-PAINTING."

"When was the last time YOU had your face → painted then, Marcus?" I ask him.

"**LAST** week, actually. I went to a

ZOMBIE PARTY - so there."

(Oh yes - I remember.)

For two days Marcus came to school with slightly

GREEN cheeks. I remind him about <u>THAT.</u>

"I wasn't <u>GREEN</u>," he says.

"You were."

"OK - but it wasn't *THAT* bad." (It was.)

"**Mr Fullerman** thought you were **ILL** and I

thought you looked **MOULDY** "

Marcus changes the subject and says ...

"Has anyone got a BETTER IDEA then?"

AMY tells everyone,

"The food stalls always do the best, but

the other groups are already making cakes

so we should do something else."

"**I** have an idea that might work," I say.

Then I take out the COMIC FOLDER.

"What do you think?"

Leroy and Solid take a look, then pass it to **AMY** and Marcus.

"This is AMAZING," **AMY** tells me.

(Thank you, thank you.)

"Using comics is a great idea!" Pansy says.

"I suppose they're OK," Marcus reluctantly agrees.

When we show them to Miss Yodel, she thinks the folders are ...

"INSPIRED!"

(Then she does that weird noise again.)

For the rest of the day, Marcus keeps on grumbling about us NOT doing FACE-PAINTING.

So I suggest that he could PAINT his own FACE to attract kids to buy the comic folders.

He doesn't seem keen. So I draw some examples for him in my sketchbook. Just an idea.

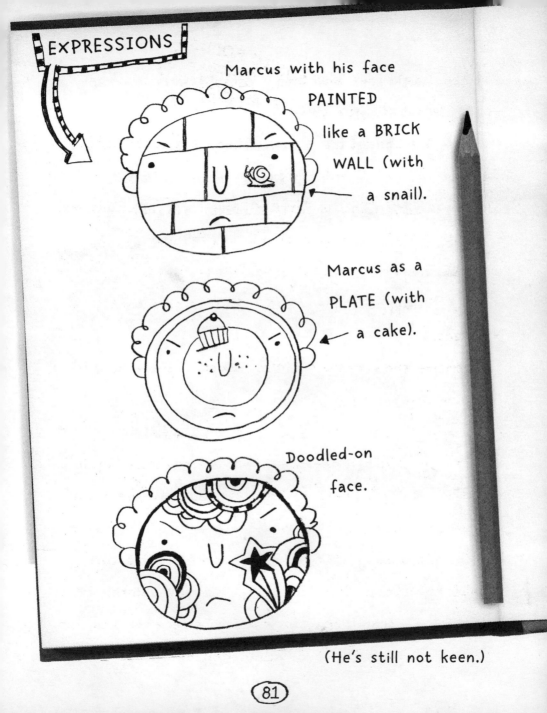

Marcus with his face PAINTED like a BRICK WALL (with a snail).

Marcus as a PLATE (with a cake).

Doodled-on face.

(He's still not keen.)

Along with Mr Fullerman, lots of kids are still off sick and not coming to school because of the **NASTY BUG** that's going around. If I could see 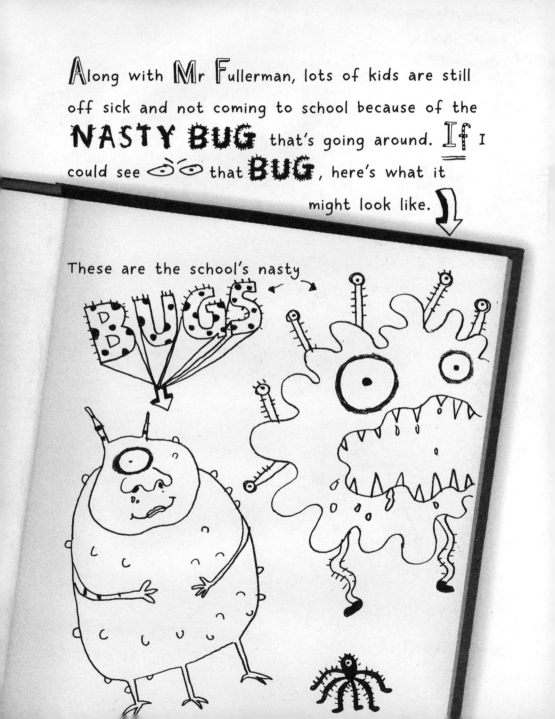 that **BUG**, here's what it might look like.

These are the school's nasty

BUGS

I'm busy drawing and not really concentrating on what Miss Yodel is saying. It sounds like she's saying something about CAKE.

HANDS UP IF YOU WOULDN'T MIND STOPPING TO HAVE CAKE.

(Which gets my ATTENTION!)

YES, PLEASE. I'll stop to have CAKE. We never have cake in class (EVER). SO I put up my hand. Then Miss Yodel THANKS me for helping out.

"Huh ... I HAVE?"

"WITH JULIA AND NOW INDRANI OFF SICK WE NEED TO EVEN OUT THE NUMBERS IN EACH BUSINESS GROUP. SO THANK YOU, TOM, FOR VOLUNTEERING TO SWAP GROUPS AND JOIN MARK CLUMP AND NORMAN WATSON."

(Oh...)

Turns out **THIS** is what Miss Yodel really said:

HANDS UP IF YOU WOULDN'T MIND SWAPPING TO THE CAKE GROUP WITH NORMAN AND MARK?

(I only heard up to the word CAKE.)

I COULD tell Miss Yodel that I've made a mistake.

But when I look over to Norman and Mark, they

look SO HAPPY, they're jumping up and down already.

"OK, Miss Yodel - I'll swap,"

I say and **AMY** nudges me.

"What did you do that for?"

"Because he's a TWIT and

didn't listen properly,"

Marcus says helpfully.

"It's true - what he said," I sigh.

Marcus seems pleased I'm moving

groups. (**AMY** looks a bit fed up.)

"Bye, then. We'll just make the comic folders without you."

Oh ... I forgot about that. I won't be able to make them now I'm not in their group. At least there'll be 🧁 cakes in my new group – which isn't SUCH a bad swap.

(I could do with a cake right now.)

Miss Yodel says I can go and sit with my new group to have a "chat" about what we're doing, which makes sense, I suppose.

When I get up to go, AMY says, "Don't worry, we'll be fine," while Marcus just WAVES at me, which is annoying.

Bye

(I wish I hadn't swapped now.)

I join Mark and Norman who want to know if they can come around to my house to make cakes. "We've never made cakes before," Mark tells me.

And I say,  "Sure – why not? How hard can it be to make a few cakes?"

So THAT'S sorted then.

Me, Norman Watson and Mark Clump will all be cooking delicious cakes for our **Business DAY SALE** at mine.

What could possibly go wrong?

Look, I'm a cake

Let's make one GIANT CAKE! Then eat it – ourselves

I have a LOT of EXPRESSIONS to draw today.

(Mostly mine.)

YES!

(When I thought I was getting cake.)

NO.

(When it turned out I wasn't.)

Maybe...

(When I found out I had to swap

business groups.)

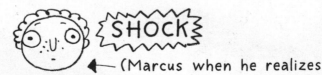← (Marcus when he realizes

that he can be a bit of an idiot.) I made that

up, but it could happen one day.

DOGZOMBIES RULE

(or would rule - if we could practise a bit more...)

Band practices haven't EXACTLY been going well lately. We can now play a WHOLE set of really good songs (well, nearly). It's getting us together that's the HARD part.

Norman's in a football team so he's been busy playing a lot of games. We never seem to be FREE at the same time. And even when we are FREE, it STILL doesn't seem to work out for us.

The last time we got together, everything was going fine until Derek's dad turned up (which isn't that unusual).

Only THIS TIME he brought June's DAD with him (which was very unusual).

Ponytail

"I thought you boys could use a few tips from a REAL musician!" Mr Fingle told us.

(Derek groaned.)

I didn't mind so much because he used to be in a BAND **(PLASTIC CUP).**

Then June's dad picked up my guitar and started to PLAY it. Mr Fingle kept saying,

I can't BELIEVE a member of **PLASTIC CUP** is ACTUALLY playing guitar in <u>MY GARAGE!</u>

Derek got really embarrassed.
He pointed out that we were in the

Dad!

middle of a REHEARSAL. But that didn't stop him.

We stuck around for a while listening to June's dad play and Derek's dad ask questions about **PLASTIC CUP.**

Look and learn, kids...

Eventually Norman had to go.

Football practice. So I asked for my guitar back, then went home as well. Bye, Derek. Later.

When I got back I told Dad all about June's dad playing my guitar so we couldn't practise that much. We tried!

Dad KEPT repeating, "WHAT? JUNE'S DAD PLAYED YOUR GUITAR? THIS GUITAR?"

"Yes, Dad – My GUITAR!" I told him a few more times.

Delia overheard us talking and BUTTED in. "What's the BIG DEAL? He's a guitarist. What do you expect him to do with a guitar?"

 (Good point, Delia, I thought – but I didn't say that out loud.)

Dad tried to explain. "Imagine if a member of **DUDE3** played your guitar, Tom. YOU'D be excited, wouldn't you?"

"YES!" I said, "Only it's NOT **DUDE3** - it's June's DAD."

"**PLASTIC CUP** were BIG in their day!" Dad said, sounding a LOT more excited than I was.

Delia sighed. "NO one's ever heard of **PLASTIC CUP** - apart from Mr Fingle and, sadly, you, Dad."

"That's not true, Delia. I bet a FAN would pay a LOT of money for Tom's guitar now June's dad's played it!"

Before Delia got any ideas I said, "I'm NOT selling my guitar."

"Mr Fingle would buy it," Delia said, laughing.

"We're keeping it," Dad said.

(Which is GOOD news for me.)

Expressions of a ~~MAD~~ music fan –
Mr Fingle. Here are the signs to look out for:

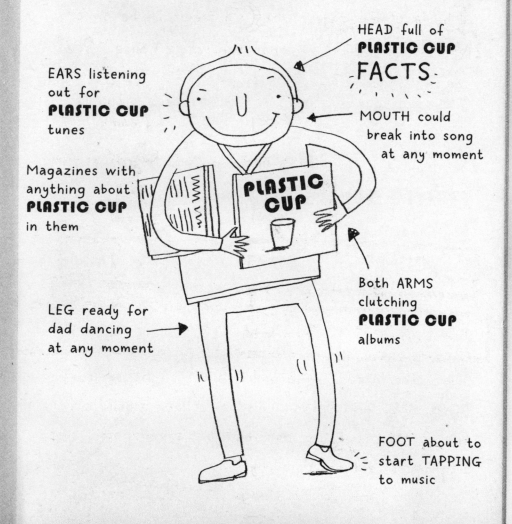

HEAD full of
PLASTIC CUP
FACTS

EARS listening
out for
PLASTIC CUP
tunes

MOUTH could
break into song
at any moment

Magazines with
anything about
PLASTIC CUP
in them

PLASTIC
CUP

Both ARMS
clutching
PLASTIC CUP
albums

LEG ready for
dad dancing
at any moment

FOOT about to
start TAPPING
to music

Where's my _ _ _ _ _ _ _ _ ?

(fill in the blank here)

In my case it could be: socks - homework - cereal

The last few days MUM seems to be on a **MISSION** to clear the whole house of any unwanted junk or stuff she thinks we don't need any more.

This mug's chipped - it's going.

I **think** it's because she's been watching **TV** programmes like:

Chuck it out!

CLEAR IT! SORT IT! SELL IT!

and

Don't be a NUTTER - Get RID of the CLUTTER.

There are boxes appearing around the house marked BOOT SALE and JUNK. This one's been sitting in the corridor outside Mum and Dad's bedroom. Dad keeps looking at everything and taking things OUT.

93

I have a look as well and find a BOX with a watch inside. I ask Dad if I can keep it. "Your mum's trying to get rid of things, Tom."

"But YOU'RE KEEPING STUFF!" I remind him.

"OK, OK," Dad says and takes the watch to have a proper look at it. Under the watch he finds something else.

"You don't want this brooch as well do you, Tom?" Then he shows me a WONKY-EYED CAT bit of jewellery.

"NO!" I say quickly and Dad laughs.

"Your mum's had this for YEARS. She's never worn it ONCE. I think it's the EYES,"

he says and pulls a face.

"Let's keep it in the box - someone might want to buy a funny-looking brooch at the boot sale."

"Maybe..." I say (or maybe NOT).

"EMPTY"

TOM'S BOX

When I come back from school the FIRST thing Mum wants to know is,

"Will you tidy your room, Tom, and find some things for the boot sale?" Then she hands me a BOX.

"OK, YES!" I say and RUN upstairs in case she gives me another job.

When Mum's in one of her

I'M SORTING THINGS OUT moods,

the best thing to do is STAY OUT OF HER WAY. I can hear drawers being emptied and cupboards opening. Hopefully I'll be SAFE up here for a while. I have a go at finding a few things for the boot sale, but it's NOT EASY ...

This one?

Maybe...

I could get rid of this comic...

Yes... Oh... No.

I haven't read it!

Still empty

... so I give up.

I'm busy reading when Mum calls from downstairs,

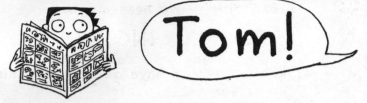

Tom!

I pretend I haven't heard her.
She'll think I'm tidying and leave me alone.

Tom!

That didn't work then. I keep quite still because
if I go downstairs she'll give me a JOB to do. Or
she'll ask me about my room (which is a bit messy).
BUT if I **don't** go downstairs, Mum will think I'm
ignoring her and she'll probably come up here and
see my messy bedroom.

WHAT should I do?

Go downstairs...

Stay here... Up... Down?

(Too late.)

"Tom, didn't you hear me

CALLING YOU?"

(I knew I should have gone downstairs.)

Mum looks around my room and says,

"I thought you said you'd tidied up, Tom?"

"I did! You should have seen it before," I tell Mum.

Then for some reason Mum *LUNGES* towards my

cupboard. And before I can stop her,

she OPENS the door.

Which is a MISTAKE.

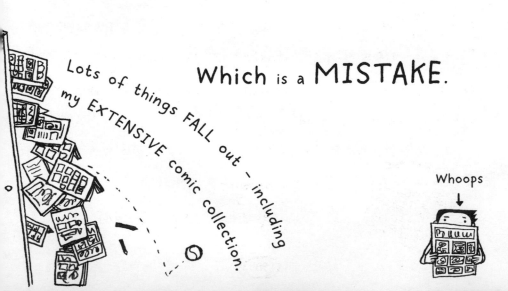

Lots of things FALL out - including my EXTENSIVE comic collection.

Whoops

"**W**hoooaaa! How many comics have you got?"

"**N**ot many," I say.

"We can sell some of these at the boot sale," Mum tells me while looking around my room again. "What else do you want to get rid of?"

I have a think...

"**N**othing from my room," I say, trying to GUARD my comics. "I need **ALL** of these for a school project." (Which is sort of true, or would be if I hadn't swapped groups.)

"**O**h, Tom, you don't have enough room to keep EVERYTHING," Mum sighs. "Just choose the comics you really want."

Which makes me **remember** something else I REALLY wanted to keep that Mum and Dad got rid of!

"I **REALLY** wanted to keep my MINI **DRUM KIT**, but THAT didn't happen," I **BLURT** OUT.

Mum looks a bit SURPRISED when I mention the MINI **DRUM KIT**. I'm NOT supposed to know what happened to it, but Delia blabbed and told me.

The MINI **DRUM KIT** was a present from Aunty Alice and Uncle Kevin, who used to encourage me to play it **ALL** the time.

Well done, Tom! Play louder!

Bang Bang

I LOVED that MINI **DRUM KIT**. Then one day I couldn't find it ANYWHERE.

Dad said, "I'm sure it will turn up soon."

BUT it never did.

Until one day I SPOTTED it inside Mum and Dad's WARDROBE! I was so PLEASED.

"Gosh ... how did that get there?" Mum said.

Look!

I started playing it STRAIGHT AWAY. It was BRILLIANT. Then it MYSTERIOUSLY went missing AGAIN.

I looked ⊙ ⊙ in ALL the same places, but couldn't find it. ☹

It was only MUCH later when I was practising my guitar (over and over as you do) that Delia STORMED into my room and told me that if I didn't STOP playing SO LOUDLY, my guitar would end up in the same place as my MINI DRUM KIT did.

THE CHARITY SHOP!

So I said,

I'll tell Mum and Dad!

and SHE said,

"Go ahead. It was Mum and Dad who took your MINI DRUM KIT there in the first place."

Which SUDDENLY explained a LOT.

The MORE I thought about my **MINI DRUM KIT**,
the MORE everything started to make SENSE.
Reminding Mum of what happened seems to have
STOPPED her from wanting to get rid of ALL
my stuff. (Phew.) ☺

 "I'm sure Uncle Kevin only bought those drums
to DRIVE us **CRAZY**, which WORKED!" Mum
tries to explain to me. Then she PROMISES I can
double-check ANYTHING she clears out.

"**OK.** PROMISE?" I say. ☺

"Promise," Mum agrees.

"Can I get another **MINI DRUM KIT** too?"

I ask hopefully.

"What do you think?"

(That'll be a **NO**, then.)

Later that evening I CATCH DELIA looking through the box outside Mum and Dad's bedroom.

HA! Caught you!

I say, which gives her a SHOCK.

"VERY funny, Tom. What's with the boxes?"

"Mum wants us all to SORT STUFF out for the BOOT SALE we're doing this weekend."

"CORRECTION - YOU'RE doing a boot sale. I'm busy."

"Mum says we ALL have to get rid of our clutter," I tell her. "It's only FAIR."

"I don't have any, so that's OK then," she says.

"I bet you do. I'll find some."

At which point Delia tells me, "STAY OUT of my room, Tom," and goes off, closing her bedroom DOOR in my FACE.

THEN I hear what sounds like a
KEY turning. That's NEW. I didn't know
DELIA could LOCK her door. I BET Mum and Dad
don't know she has a key.

I PRESS my ear to her door and keep listening.

GO AWAY!

she shouts at me. So I stay very still.

I can hear you...
Get lost.

I hold my breath and sit down.

I'm not opening the door,

she says. But I stay where I am and
listen a bit more. I try looking through
the keyhole, but she's left
the KEY inside.

Delia's UP to something. I can TELL.
I hang around for a bit longer, until I get bored.

Is Delia an ALIEN? (Maybe...)

The next morning, I'm tucking into my cereal when in walks Delia. I don't mention her LOCKED DOOR. (I'll save that one for later.)

Instead I CONCENTRATE on the SQUISHED cereal from my school bag that I've left out in the HOPE she MIGHT have it for her breakfast.

Which would be FUNNY!

"HELP yourself," I say casually, like I don't really care. (I do.)

SHE PICKS it UP. (YES!)

Then she puts it DOWN. (No...)

"Changed my mind. Bad luck, Tom," Delia says. (How did she know? It's like she's some kind of ALIEN with special powers to SENSE STUFF.) Maybe THAT'S why she's been locking her door...

(104) Alien → Hello!

I hold that thought for my sketchbook and
CHANGE the subject to see what ELSE Delia KNOWS.
"So do you know what's happening NEXT
weekend?" I ask her.

"It's Mum's birthday. Did you forget?"
she asks, helping herself to toast.
"NO... I was going to tell YOU it was
Mum's birthday."

"But you did forget," Delia says, which is
annoying.
"Dad forgot - NOT ME!"

"What did he forget NOW?" Mum asks as she walks
into the kitchen. She's not wearing her
normal work clothes.
"NOTHING," I say, trying to cover up as
Dad is standing just behind her.
"I'm sorting everything out today -
including your SHED," she tells Dad.

105

What?

"There must be LOADS to get rid of in there," Mum says like she means it.

"NO, nothing," Dad says quickly.

"What about that old piece of GYM equipment that you NEVER use?"

"I use it EVERY DAY!" Dad tells her.

"Hanging your hat and jacket on it doesn't count." Mum shakes her head.

"You said I didn't use it – you didn't say WHAT FOR!" Dad laughs.

(I'm worried about MY ROOM now because Mum looks like she's going into BATTLE!)

So before I go to school, I run upstairs and STICK NOTES on all the things I don't want her to TOUCH.

JUST IN CASE.

Books and comics

Don't touch

Pile of clothes

KEEP

ANYTHING with DUDE3

Hands OFF

NO

All guitars

Massive shoes

SELL!

It's hard to concentrate at school while I'm wondering WHAT Mum might be doing in my room.

As soon as the bell goes, I tell Derek I'm in a BIG *hurry* to get home and see what's left of my stuff.

When I open the front door it looks different already. I head upstairs and notice Delia's door is STILL SHUT (and probably locked).

Which is suspicious (for lots of reasons).

I go into my room ... and it's SO ☆T☆IDY☆ WOW! I hardly recognize it.

"Doesn't it look better already?" Mum says.

I double-check what she's put in the "FOR BOOT SALE" box before I say, "Yes, Mum. It looks great."

Mum says that if anything gets sold from MY box, I get to keep the  money. 🙂 "Well ... MOST of the money," she adds, which is better than nothing, I suppose. I'm HOPING I might have enough to buy something like a MINI scooter. (Loads of kids at school have them.) OR EVEN

ONE HUNDRED

CARAMEL WAFERS

(Imagine 100) → That would be good! 🙂

I'm actually looking forward to doing this BOOT SALE now. Right up until Mum reminds me what time I have to get up in the morning.

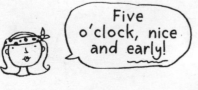
Five o'clock, nice and early!

Groan

(I stay up a bit later than I should doing some important drawings in my sketchbook – mostly inspired by Delia.)

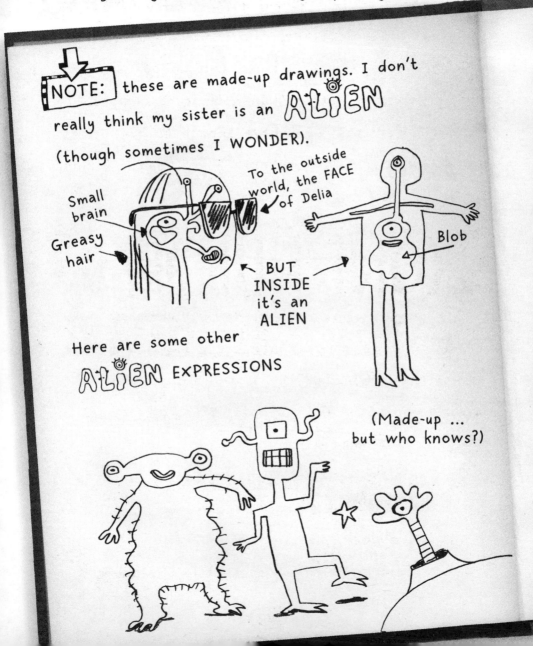

NOTE: these are made-up drawings. I don't really think my sister is an ALIEN (though sometimes I WONDER).

Small brain

Greasy hair

To the outside world, the FACE of Delia

BUT INSIDE it's an ALIEN

Blob

Here are some other ALIEN EXPRESSIONS

(Made-up ... but who knows?)

DING! DING! DING!

THAT'S the alarm that Mum gave me so I'd wake up for the BOOT SALE this morning going off. (It worked.) It's SO EARLY it doesn't feel like I've been asleep at all. ⊙ ⊙

The alarm's WOKEN Delia up too. I can hear her **COMPLAINING** and telling me to,

"Turn that thing OFF!"

So I let it ring just a little bit longer.

DING! DING! DING! DING!

(OK, that's enough now.)

I leap out of bed and get dressed as quickly as I can. Then I leave the alarm clock outside Delia's door and set it to go off again at SIX A.M.

5:40

(Just after we've gone.)

Ha! Ha! 6:00

Mum and Dad are already downstairs. They look quite tired.

Have you got the change?

Yup!

Dad holds up a utility belt and shakes it around.

"A pen for writing signs?"

"YES, it's ALL sorted," Dad says.

"RIGHT, LET'S GO!" Mum says, being all enthusiastic.

(Groan...)

Mum and Dad get into the front of the car

while I'm squashed in the back, surrounded by boxes.

I can't see anything that belongs to Delia, not

even a **ROCK WEEKLY** (which is a shame).

I ask Mum, "How come Delia didn't have to

get rid of anything?"

Mum says, "I couldn't get into her room. The

door was STUCK."

"Or maybe it was LOCKED," I tell

her helpfully. "I heard her using a KEY the other

day."

"When did she get a key?" Dad asks while

fiddling with his own car keys.

"Why does Delia need to LOCK her bedroom door?" Mum wonders.

"You'll have to talk to her," Mum tells Dad.

"WHY me?"

"Come to think of it, I smelt PAINT in her room the other day. I hope she's not redecorating or anything silly like that. Can we GO?" Mum asks Dad in a slightly irritated voice.

"Ok, OK, the engine's just warming up. Ready now."

Mum turns round and says to me,

"This is EXCITING, isn't it, Tom?"

"Not really," I sigh.

Then Dad tries to start the car, but there's a problem...

NOTHING HAPPENS.

So he turns the key again ...

and this time there's a LOUD CLUNKING NOISE.

Which doesn't sound good. 🙁

Dad keeps turning the key ON and OFF ... ON and OFF ... ON and OFF...

He's pressing the pedals a lot too. Nothing seems to be working. "It's completely dead," Dad says.

He **SHAKES** the steering wheel.

"Is that going to help?" Mum sighs.

"WHY does this car <u>ALWAYS</u> break down?" Dad says, resting his head on the wheel.

"Uncle Kevin says it's because it's a REALLY **OLD** car. I think he called it 'clapped out'," I tell them from the back seat.

"Thanks for sharing that, Tom," Dad says, trying the keys again.

"PLEASE tell me we can get this car working?" Mum asks hopefully.

"Does this mean I can go back to bed?" Which seems like a sensible thing to ask under the circumstances.

"WE'RE DOING THIS BOOT SALE one way or another."

"Just asking," I say. Mum sounds VERY determined.

"The Fingles are away for the weekend, so we can't ask them," Dad says, thinking out loud.

"How about our new neighbours?" Mum wonders.

Dad points out that they don't have a car.

"Would your brother Kevin be able to help us out?" Mum suggests.

"ARE YOU KIDDING ME? I'd never hear the END of it. He'd drive me CRAZY!" Dad says.

(He's going a bit CRAZY himself.)

All the time they're chatting I'm still squished up in the back seat.

"OK, I've got an idea," Mum says, which sounds hopeful.

"I'll give Mavis a call. She's always up early because Bob snores so much."

SNNNOORE
SNOORE

I'm WONDERING why Mum's ringing THE FOSSILS when they don't have a car. Maybe they know someone at the LEAFY GREEN OLD FOLK'S HOME who does?

Take it for a spin!

I can hear Mum on the phone talking to Granny. She says, "Fantastic! Thanks, Mavis. We owe you."

Mum starts to unload the car. Which is a GOOD SIGN.

So I get out as well and ask, "Are Granny Mavis and Granddad Bob coming with another car then?"

Mum says, "Not exactly."

(I wasn't expecting that.)

Their small trailer is just big enough to fit most of the boxes.

There are a few bags that we have to carry. We get some funny looks on the way to the boot sale but at least we get there (eventually).

All the good spots have gone by the time we arrive. The man taking the money says, "This is the only place you can have, I'm afraid." It's right in the corner of the car park.

"It's better than nothing," Mum says, looking around.

"Right! Let's get cracking or we'll never sell anything," Dad tells us.

"Where's the table to put everything on?" Mum wonders.

"What table?" Dad says.

(Dad's forgotten the table.)

I stay out of the way while they work out what to use instead.

(The trailer + upturned boxes with trays on top.)

My tummy's RUMBLING so when Granddad suggests we should go and grab some breakfast for everyone I say,

"YES, PLEASE!" really fast.

Granny Mavis tells Granddad, "Healthy breakfasts. Remember, Bob?"

"Of course!" he says, patting his stomach, and off we go.

The great thing about a BOOT SALE is you NEVER know what you're going to find. ☺

I see all kinds of strange things on the different stalls, like a BIG slipper (Granddad likes that), funny books and a mini scooter.

Mini scooter

"Oh, Granddad! I really want to get a mini scooter."

"Let's have a look."

The scooter's almost new, so the stallholder wants more money than we've got. (I don't have any. YET.)

"We can come back later," Granddad says.

"You might get it cheaper then..." he whispers to me so the stallholder can't hear.

The smell of breakfast takes my mind off the scooter for a bit. Granddad orders fresh orange juice and THICK slices of toast with jam to take back for everyone.

I can't help looking at all the CAKES and BUNS and thinking how tasty they'd be when Granddad says, "Shall we get something to eat HERE?"

"Good idea!" I nod. "😊" But then he orders...

"Two vegetarian breakfasts, please."

😕 (Not cake.)

Which turns out to be CHIPS! (Yeah!)

"Don't mention this to your granny," he tells me.

OK!

By the time we get back, Mum and Dad (with Granny's help) have set up the stall, which looks better than I thought it would. Apart from ALL THE WEIRD STUFF.

"What's with the odd costumes everywhere?" I ask.

"You remember me wearing the dinosaur one, don't you, Tom?"

(Oh, yes. It's all coming back to me now.)

"These are from different jobs I've done. They're attracting attention to the stall already," Dad explains to me.

He's right. People are STARING 👀

(but not in a good way).

Look at those freaky boots!

It feels like HALF my school are at the boot sale, because EVERY TIME I look up there's someone else I know walking past. Probably thinking,

What a WEIRD-looking stall.

Then they spot ME standing there. Like Brad Galloway's just done. He starts waving. So I wave back.

Oh, great. There are some of the little kids who beat me at Champ too.

I wave some more - but NOT very enthusiastically.

Granddad starts handing around the toast, which is a nice distraction. I'm not really that hungry after the chips so I just have my juice while Granddad manages to eat a small piece of toast.

"Is that **ALL** you're having, Bob?" Granny asks.

"Don't worry about ME. I'll be fine. There wasn't enough toast for everyone," he says, trying to make Granny feel sorry for him (which works).

"We'll get something else for you to eat later," she tells him.

"Like CHIPS!" Granddad suggests, then winks at me.

"We'll see," Granny says.

I keep quiet about the **LARGE** portion of chips we both had earlier.

Granddad is one sneaky **OLD FOSSIL**, that's for sure. **Ha! Ha!**

I might even let you share them...

EVERYWHERE seems to be busy now...
apart from our stall.

(Or that's what it feels like.)
"I think your GLITTER boots
are keeping people away," Mum tells Dad.
"I'll never get a chance to look around at this rate,"
she adds, trying to rearrange things.
"I'll do that. You go off and EVERYTHING
will be sold by the time you come back. Won't it,
Tom?"

"Maybe?" I say, because I'm not sure THAT's
going to happen.

Dad manages to assure Mum that we'll be fine.
So she goes to have a little browse.

"Right! Come on, Tom," Dad says, rubbing his hands
together. "Let's put all these boxes out, shall we?"
The stall looks a bit messy but, surprisingly, it
seems to be working.

More
Stuff

People begin to come over and start BUYING our STUFF! Someone even wants Dad's

GLITTER BOOTS – which cheers him up. ☺

I'm feeling a lot happier as well when **B**rad Galloway comes over and shows me what he's bought.

"Hi, Tom. Check out my **GIANT** water slide."

"That's **BRILLIANT!** I've always wanted one of those," I tell him.

"I WISH I could bring this to school and set it up at break time," Brad says. "How good would that be?"

"**SO GOOD!** Though I'd probably end up sliding into one of the teachers, knowing my luck," I say. Which is true... (I can see it now.)

LOOK OUT!

Mr Fullerman →

Brad laughs and says, "That reminds me. I nearly BUMPED into Mrs Nap. Marcus Meldrew is here as well."

"Is there anyone from our school who ISN'T here?" I wonder. Who knew boot sales were so popular?

We're still chatting when an old lady wearing a headscarf comes over and picks up the box with Mum's CROSS-EYED CAT brooch inside.

"What do you want for this?" she asks.

Dad jumps in immediately and says, "Let me see. What do you think, Tom?"

I have a look and say as confidently as I can, "At LEAST five pounds. It's a special cat."

The old lady puts it down straight away.

"I'll think about it."

"TWO POUNDS THEN!" Dad shouts, doing his best to convince her.

"Maybe..." she says and carries on looking.
While she's making up her mind, Brad spots Marcus
Meldrew, who's coming over to see us.

 "What are you doing here?" he asks me.

"Selling ice cream. What do you think?"

"You've got ice cream?"

"No, Marcus. We're selling house
stuff. Like you do at a boot sale."

"Look what I've got." Brad shows him the
water slide.

"That's good. Have you got anything like that,
Tom?" he asks me.

No.

Marcus looks disappointed. Brad decides NOW is a
good time for him to go.

"See you at school," he says and leaves me
with Marcus. Who picks up the box the old lady was
looking at and SHAKES it. A LOT.

"What's in here?"

"A cat brooch that's probably broken now you've shaken it so much," I tell him.

"I hope not. I want to buy it!" the old lady suddenly says, after seeing what Marcus is doing.

Marcus hands over the box while Dad is hovering around, HOPING she's ready to buy it THIS TIME.

"Will you take a pound?" the old lady asks.

"DONE!" Dad says before she changes her mind. The old lady looks VERY pleased with the brooch.

"One more thing SOLD," Dad says.

"Great," I say, while watching Marcus, who's RUMMAGING through ALL of my stuff and asking questions about EVERYTHING. SIGH...

"Is this book any good?"

"Yes, it's a great book."

"Why are you selling it then?"

"Because I've read it."

"What size is this T-shirt?"

"My size."

"What's this?"

"A GAME."

"Have you got any other games?"

He's driving me CRAZY.

Dad comes to my rescue and shows Marcus a few

other things he thinks he might like.

"It's a kite I made. We need to

get rid of EVERYTHING here,

Marcus, so keep looking," Dad tells him.

(I can see something I'd like to get rid of

right NOW.)

Marcus carries on

RUMMAGING

around our stall when

Mum comes

CHARGING back.

Nuisance

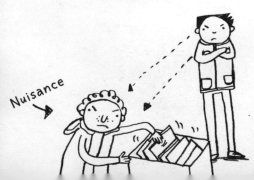

She's all out of breath and PUFFING.

"I've just seen your Aunty Alice and Uncle Kevin wandering around. Who on EARTH told them we were doing a BOOT SALE?"

(Errr... That might have been me?)

Hi, Aunty Alice. Mum's not in. We're doing a boot sale this Sunday. Yes, a BOOT SALE. THIS SUNDAY.

Mum is in a right PANIC.

"Quick! Hide ALL these mugs and that VASE they gave us. I don't want them to see that we're trying to SELL THEM!" she shouts while Dad helps her SHOVE them into a BOX.

"What's going on?" Marcus asks me, because he's <u>STILL</u> here.

"Nothing. Don't worry about it."

(He's just being nosy.) "Are you going to buy something?" I ask him.

"I haven't decided yet," he tells me. Mum has started to calm down and SPOTS Marcus, who's looking at my COMICS.

"Hello, Marcus.

Do you like comics? Tom's got FAR too many, as you can see."

"Not any MORE, I don't," I remind her.

"Actually THESE comics would be REALLY useful for MY **Business DAY** project. But I don't think I have enough money."

He's looking at the money in his hand really sadly.

(No money)

(He's so annoying.)

132

OH WELL, NEVER MIND. SEE YOU AT SCHOOL THEN, MARCUS.

I say, trying to get rid of him. But Mum has

already started to put my comics into a BAG.

"You'll be doing us BOTH a favour, Marcus.

HERE, JUST TAKE THEM **ALL**."

"WHAT?"

Before I can stop Mum or say ANYTHING, she's

given the WHOLE LOT AWAY.

"Thanks, Mrs Gates. That's brilliant. This will

really help MY **business group**'s

idea. Won't it, Tom?"

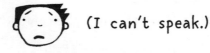

(I can't speak.)

Mum's smiling and says to me, "One less thing for us to take home, which is good news and why we're here in the first place, Tom!"

AND I WANT TO SHOUT "IT'S TERRIBLE NEWS and not good at ALL!"

But I'm still speechless.

I have to look at Marcus being all smug and thanking my mum for the comics as he finally leaves our stall. smug I'm just about to say something to Mum about WHY she gave ALL my comics AWAY

when she =NUDGES me and says, "Uh-oh! Here comes Alice, Kevin and the boys. Don't mention the mugs! Just act NORMALLY."

While not acting normally at all.  HI!

"Well, look at you ALL. How's it going? Made your first **MILLION** yet?"

Uncle Kevin says, which has already annoyed Dad.

"Hilarious," he mutters.

My cousins are eating HOT Doughnuts and they *smell* amazing.

(The Doughnuts, <u>not</u> my cousins.)

"Those Doughnuts look good," I

say, hoping one of the cousins might offer me one.

Which would REALLY help take my mind OFF Marcus

getting ALL my COMICS for FREE. ☹

"They WERE delicious. We've eaten them all."

"Oh..."

(Today just gets better and better ... not.)

Aunty Alice is looking around our stall. She turns to Uncle Kevin and says, "This is SUCH a good idea. We should do a BOOT SALE as well."

"What with? We don't have any JUNK to sell."

(Now Mum's annoyed.)

"It's NOT JUNK, Kevin. It's just some things we don't need any more," she tells him. Uncle Kevin picks up one of Dad's old funny hats.

"I can see why this isn't useful any more!"

"Someone else might find it useful – that's the WHOLE point," Mum adds. "Look, I've just bought these EARRINGS that somebody didn't need, but they're just right for me." She takes out two small earrings with CATS on them and blue stones around the sides.

"I thought we were getting rid of STUFF, not buying MORE?" Dad points out.

"We are! But ..."

Here we go, Dad says, waiting for Mum's excuse.

"... THESE are the PERFECT match to go with my great-great-grandmother's JEWELLED cat brooch."

Dad and I say nothing.

"I keep meaning to get its EYES fixed at a good jewellers. Especially as it has REAL DIAMONDS and SAPPHIRES on the COLLAR."

"Diamonds..." Dad repeats.

"Are you sure?"

"Does that mean it's worth LOADS of money, then?" I ask and Dad gives me a LOOK.

"I think I saw something similar on ANTIQUE TREASURES."

(I think we've just made a **MASSIVE** mistake.)

"Are you OK, Frank? You look like you've seen a GHOST," Uncle Kevin says.

"I'm FINE," Dad manages to say.

(But he doesn't look fine.)

"So there you go, Kevin. These earrings aren't JUNK. They'll go beautifully with my CAT brooch."

"Hey! Maybe you could SELL the cat brooch and buy a car that doesn't break down all the time!" Uncle Frank jokes, pointing at the mobility scooter.

"The car's already being fixed," Mum says sternly. "NO ONE is selling MY brooch. I LOVE IT! It's at home, somewhere SAFE."

(I wish it was...)

I keep quiet while Dad whispers to me,
"We have to find that old lady!"

All this time my cousins have been looking around our stall. They pull out a box and start searching through it.

"Hey, LOOK! We've got the same MUGS as these at home, don't we?" Mum GRABS the box really quickly and says, "What are THEY doing here? They're not for sale."

Then shoves it back out of the way before Aunty Alice or Uncle Kevin realize what they are.

"Why don't you all go and have a look around the rest of the boot sale while you're here?" she suggests.

"Great idea," Dad agrees.

Uncle Kevin PATS Dad on the back as they leave. "Good luck selling the rest of the JUNK!" he laughs. (Dad isn't laughing.)

"And I thought today couldn't get any worse," Dad says to me.

"Right! I'm going to FIND that old lady and get it BACK," Dad tells me quietly, so Mum can't hear.

"OK," I say.

 "Take this tenner, Tom, and if you see her walk past, give it to her and tell her what's happened. DON'T mention the diamonds though... We want her to give it back."

"YES, Dad," I say and put the money in my pocket.

"What are you two *WHISPERING* about?" Mum wants to know.

"NOTHING!"

we both say, a bit too quickly.

"I was just going to find Mum and Dad and make sure they're OK," Dad says, which is SMART thinking.

Dad runs off into the crowd of people and I keep watch from our stall just in case she comes back.

Mum is busy selling and chatting to anyone who comes over. Which is just as well because if she SAW the way Dad's CHARGING around the BOOT SALE she might get suspicious!

I'm doing my best to try and spot the old lady as well. So far all I've seen is Dad run past me four times. Then, all of a SUDDEN, I see a lady with a headscarf standing RIGHT opposite our stall. That's her! I'm SURE it is.

I tell Mum, "I NEED to look at that stall over there - RIGHT NOW!"

"OK, Tom. Calm down. Just stay where I can see you," she tells me.

The old lady hasn't moved. I'm about to RUSH over when Mum stops me.

"HANG ON! - Wait, Tom."

(What NOW?) "Mum, I have to HURRY!"

"Don't you want some of the money you've made in case you see something?" she asks me.

"Oh ... yes, please."

Mum hands over a few pounds, which I wasn't expecting. I turn around and push my way through the crowd until I get to the old lady in the scarf. She's chatting to someone else and still has her back to me. Dad is going to be SO PLEASED!

I tap her on the back and say ...

Hello, Tom. It's me, Mrs Nap. I don't have your cat brooch, I'm afraid.

(Brad didn't tell me Mrs Nap was wearing a SCARF!)

Oh NO – this is embarrassing.

"Sorry, Mrs Nap. I thought you were an old lady," I tell her.

"Thanks, Tom. I do feel like an old lady after a week of teaching sometimes!"

I'm slightly distracted by a cuckoo clock that catches my eye. I've always wanted a cuckoo clock. I wonder if it works?

"I hope you find the cat brooch, Tom," Mrs Nap says to me.

(Oh yes ... the CAT BROOCH.)

"Me too," I say, while looking a bit more at the clock. "Thanks, Mrs Nap. My dad's looking for the old lady as well. I'm not sure if we'll find her. There's so many people here."

"Good luck, Tom," Mrs Nap says as she walks away.

I ask how much the clock is... It's a BARGAIN!

"**W**hat's that?" Mum asks when I get back.

"A cuckoo clock. I think it works,"

I tell her cheerfully.

"Do you REALLY need a cuckoo clock, Tom?"

"**YES!** I really do," I say. (Who doesn't?)

"Where are you going to put it?" she wants

to know.

"I have **LOADS** of **FREE** space where

my **comics** USED to be," I remind Mum. (I'm STILL

not HAPPY about giving them to Marcus.)

"And it will make a MUCH nicer sound than the

ALARM CLOCK 12:30 you gave me."

(Which is true.)

I'm **EXCITED** to show Dad my new clock

when he comes back.

"You'll never guess what I've found!" I say

when I see him and Dad gives me a

GREAT BIG HUG.

"Well done, Tom, you CLEVER BOY!" (Which is nice.)

"**I** THOUGHT we'd LOST it for GOOD. Let's have a look then." He seems more excited than I am about my cuckoo clock. Until I show it to him.

"WHAT'S THAT?"

"A cuckoo clock," I say. (Why doesn't anyone know what a cuckoo clock looks like?)

"I thought you'd found ... you-know-WHAT," he sighs.

"Oh, sorry. I did see an old lady in a scarf but it turned out to be Mrs Nap," I explain.

"That happened to me as well. I have no idea where the old lady's gone now," Dad says.

I don't have the cat brooch.

"Are you still looking for Bob and Mavis?" Mum overhears our conversation and thinks Dad is still trying to find **THE FOSSILS**. So he plays along...

"Yes, I looked EVERYWHERE. They've completely disappeared into THIN AIR. I don't know WHERE they've gone to," Dad says.

"That's funny – because I can see them from here." Mum says then points at ...

... **THE FOSSILS**, who are finishing off some chips.

(<u>MORE</u> chips in Granddad's case)

With the boot sale nearly finished and NO sign of the OLD lady with the brooch ANYWHERE, we all start to pack up and get ready to go home.

Granddad says he's sorry I didn't get the mini scooter after all. I told him it was fine because

NOW I have a CUCKOO clock (and a bouncy ball, but I didn't show that to Mum).

Granny and Granddad take their mobility scooter back home and we carry the last few bags and boxes to the charity shop.

(Including the mugs and vase.)

"Alice and Kevin don't go to charity shops. They won't see them in here," Mum says.

"I hope you're right – or I'll **N**EVER hear the end of it," Dad says.

"They might see them if they get put in the window," I point out. "Like when I saw my MINI **DRUM KIT**," I add, just to remind Mum and Dad that I know what really happened.

"You'll understand when you're older," Dad tells me. Mum and Dad both think I've been really good today so I'm allowed to get a couple of cartoon films I SPOT in the charity shop. **AND** because we're all really tired, we get the bus home. I'm sitting on the top of the bus and Dad says quietly to me, "I might need to find another brooch to replace it. Because the chances of seeing that old lady again aren't great, Tom."

"I'll keep looking," I say.

"You never know, Dad. She could be anywhere."

When we get home, Delia's still in her room.

"Can you smell paint? I can smell paint."

"I can't," Dad says, collapsing into a chair.

"You should go and talk to Delia
about paint and locked doors," Mum tells Dad.

"Do I have to? Can't it WAIT?"

"I suppose so," Mum sighs.

So I go and have a CHAT with her instead.

"Do you want to see my NEW CLOCK?"
I shout, knocking on her door.

"NO," she shouts back.

"What are you doing?" I ask.

"Go away, Tom. And <u>don't</u> leave your alarm clock
outside my room again or it might get **BROKEN**."

(I forgot I did that! Ha! Ha!)

I go to my room and decide to TEST my new clock
by moving the hands on to EVERY HOUR to see if
it works.

 **CUCKOO**   It DOES!

It's LOUD too. So LOUD Delia can hear it.

So I do it again ... and again!

SKETCHBOOK

Here are some sketches INSPIRED by the boot sale today.

My SNEAKY granddad pretending NOT to have eaten CHIPS

What CHIPS?

Chip EVIDENCE

Dad when he got a SURPRISE. (NOT a good one. I can't say what it was.)

NO!

CLOSE-UP of EYES
After early morning wake-up call.

Delia – being impressed with my cuckoo clock.

CUCKOO

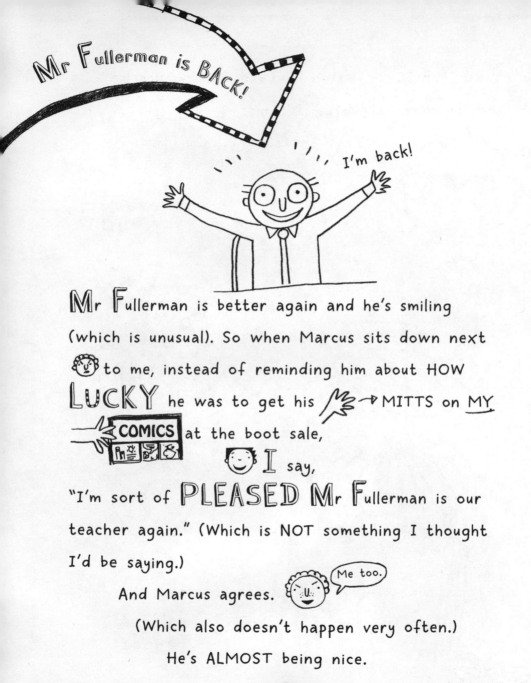

Mr Fullerman is BACK!

I'm back!

Mr Fullerman is better again and he's smiling (which is unusual). So when Marcus sits down next to me, instead of reminding him about HOW LUCKY he was to get his MITTS on MY COMICS at the boot sale, I say,

"I'm sort of PLEASED Mr Fullerman is our teacher again." (Which is NOT something I thought I'd be saying.)

And Marcus agrees. Me too.

(Which also doesn't happen very often.)

He's ALMOST being nice.

Then for SOME reason he takes me by surprise and decides to HIGH FIVE me.

But he keeps MISSING my hand.

Huh?

High five.

This is AWKWARD.

His HIGH FIVE ends up being more like a ...

low three.

"Are you deliberately being a TWIT, Tom?" Marcus asks me, like it was MY fault.

I'm glad when Mr Fullerman starts doing the school register. 😟

"GOOD MORNING, CLASS 5F. NICE TO SEE YOU ALL."

"Good Morning, Mr Fullerman,"

we reply in a REALLY nice, BRIGHT, cheery kind of way. ☺

"I hope you were THIS polite and well behaved for Miss Yodel," he adds.

(Hmmmm. Sort of.)

Mr Fullerman tells us he's going to come around and have a quick CATCH-UP CHAT with all of us to make sure we're ready for our Business DAY!

"I'm SO ready," Marcus says.

"Me too," I say. (I'm not really.)

When Mr Fullerman gets to our table, I have to listen to Marcus telling him all about HIS idea for the comic folders.

"Did Marcus just say it was HIS idea to make comic folders?" I ask AMY, just to check I wasn't hearing things.

"Yup, that's what he said," AMY replies.

Mr Fullerman has already spoken to Mark and Norman, so he knows what I'm doing and says, **"I'm looking forward to trying one of your delicious CAKES, Tom."**

(Ha! He says that NOW.)

When Mr Fullerman goes back to his desk I say to Marcus, "Your idea, Marcus?"

"It doesn't matter whose idea it was. We're all working together to raise money," Marcus says.

(TRUE ... but ANNOYING.)

All that stuff I said about missing **Mr Fullerman** . . . I TAKE IT BACK. Because NOW that he's feeling BETTER he's making us **work** a **LOT**. It's like **Mr Fullerman** has got his **SUPERHUMAN** hearing and seeing **POWERS** back too.

"Put away the comic, Tom, I can see it behind the book."

He's just pointed to a stack of worksheets and told us, **"Today we'll be working our way through THESE. I thought this would be a FUN topic for you ALL to do."**

(Fun ... is he kidding?

It's SUCH a **BIG** pile.)

Then he hands them out.

MYTHS, LEGENDS and FAIRY TALES

This is your chance to write a MYTH, LEGEND or FAIRY TALE.

Think about the style of the stories we've been reading like Robin Hood and Little Red Riding Hood.
- Think about WHERE your story is set.
- Include some interesting CHARACTERS.
- Give it a great BEGINNING, fantastic MIDDLE and brilliant ENDING.

You may finish this off as homework if you don't get it done today. Have fun!

Mr Fullerman

Phew... That's not so bad after all. I'm going to write a story about a VERY ANNOYING TROLL who nicks other people's ideas.

(Good thinking!)

I'm starting to write it when I get distracted by imagining 'what' the troll would look like.

(I'm getting inspiration from everywhere.)

Then I spend such a LONG time drawing my troll, I run out of time to write my story.

Mr Fullerman says I have to finish it at home now.

Oh well, never mind.

Here's my troll. Remind you of anyone?

The annoying TROLL who thought he was right about everything.

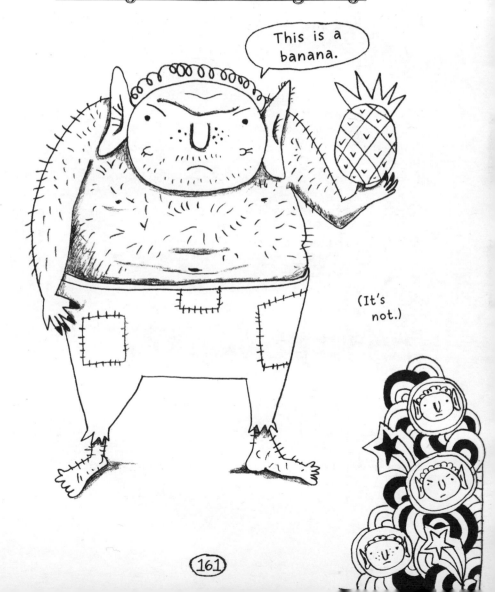

This is a banana.

(It's not.)

When I get home, Dad is stomping around our slightly LESS cluttered house.

"Hi, Dad," I say and ══ *THROW* my school bag down.

Dad is holding a bit of paper and WAVING it around which makes me {THINK} I might be in trouble.

"Hi, Tom. Do you know how much our car is going to cost to get fixed?" he asks me.

(At least it's NOT about me then!)

I shrug my shoulders and take a WILD guess.

"A MILLION pounds?"

"You're not far off. It's going to cost a fortune just to get that old rust bucket back on the road. We might as well get a new car."

"YEAH! Let's get a NEW CAR!" I agree.

"We could only afford an AN OLD banger but we have one of those already. What with this AND losing Mum's brooch..." Dad sighs.

He looks a bit stressed. So I don't remind him that we didn't really *LOSE* it - we <u>SO</u>LD it for ONE POUND. I try and CHEER him up with a GOOD suggestion.

"Maybe you could get your OWN mobility scooter for EMERGENCIES?"

Which makes Dad laugh.

"Give it a few years, Tom," he says, then adds, "That reminds me. I FOUND another form of transport HIDING in my shed that I thought we could use. Do you want to come and have a go?"

"YES, PLEASE!" I say, because this sounds like it could be FUN ...

SKETCHBOOK

My mum's expressions when she's racing Dad on the spacehopper

(Mum won)

Delia not being impressed

Me, embarrassed at Mum's lap of honour

Rooster being a dog

Business DAY

(Not today. Tomorrow.)

Mr Fullerman is checking if we're all ready and set for tomorrow. He says,

> **We're going to raise the MOST MONEY EVER, AREN'T WE, CLASS 5F?**

"**Yeah!**" we all cheer. And next door Mr Sprocket's class cheers at EXACTLY the same time as we do.

Yeah!

So Mr Fullerman says,

"I CAN'T HEAR YOU, CLASS 5F?"

(Like it's a cheering competition ...)

"YEAH!"

(... that we win.) ☺

AMY and Marcus and the rest of their group have made the **COMIC** folders.

I ask Marcus, "Can I see one?"

"Hands off! Don't mess them up, Tom," he snaps at me.

AMY ignores him and shows me a folder anyway.

"What do you think?" she asks me.

"They look great, **AMY**. Nice to see all **MY** old comics being used again."

"Your comics? Marcus told us they were HIS comics."

So I explain... ➡

"They were my comics, then my mum gave them to Marcus."

"So that makes them MINE," Marcus adds.

(Which is true - but they WERE mine.)

"I was selling them at the boot sale, anyway," I explain.

"Oh YES, I SAW you there," **AMY** says.

"You DID?"

"Yes, me and Florence watched you TAPPING Mrs Nap on the back and then chatting to her for AGES," **AMY** tells me.

"It's a **LONG** story."

I try and explain when Marcus BUTTS in to say, "**NO**, it's not. I know what happened. Tom only went and SOLD his mum's special, **expensive**, OLD brooch for - wait for it - **ONE POUND**. He was begging to get it back."

"From Mrs Nap?"

"I thought she was the old lady who bought the brooch. They looked similar – it was a mistake."

(This is getting complicated.)

"Does your mum know you sold her precious brooch for only ONE POUND yet?" Marcus asks me.

"NO – and she's not going to find out because I'm going to get it back," I say sternly.

"I bet you don't."

"I will. You'll see."

(I might not – but Marcus doesn't need to know that.)

AMY actually sticks up for me and says, "Give it a REST, Marcus. Tom might find it. You never know."

"There's not much chance of that," says Marcus.

"That's what you think," I tell him, getting the last word in before Norman and Mark come and see me about OUR plans for making cakes.

HI!

So far our PLAN is MAKE CAKES. That's it. 🙂

Mark wants to know if he can bring his pet SNAKE over  to mine, which is a good question.

I have a think about it.   Hmmm...

Delia would probably FREAK OUT if she saw a REAL snake in the house.

HI!

Mum and Dad might not be too happy either.

Snake   Snake

It could all end in CHAOS.

So I tell Mark,

OF COURSE you can bring your snake. Why not? It will be FUN!

(Fingers crossed.)

The rest of my day makes my  BRAIN HURT.

MATHS is not my best subject and, worse still, everyone else looks like they understand WHAT Mr Fullerman is saying. (I don't.)

I put on my special "I'm concentrating" face and think about other things instead. Like CAKES. I draw a few different types that would be BRILLIANT to sell ... and EAT.

Whole wafers

GIANT cake

Wafers

Monster cake

IF ONLY

It takes up just enough time to get to the end of the lesson.

Walking home

Derek tells me all about what his group have made.

Which sounds EXCELLENT.

It's a TREASURE ISLAND GAME and the PRIZE is a treasure chest STUFFED FULL of good treats.

All you have to do is guess WHERE the treasure is buried.

"Do you know where it is?" I ask Derek.

"Nope. Haven't a clue!" (Which is a shame.)

Tom

(You write your name on a flag then press it on to a square on the treasure map.)

Sand and model island

Mum is still at work when I get home. But she's left a NOTE

Hi Tom,
Dad will help you make biscuits.
Love, Mum x

BISCUITS? What happened to making CAKES?

I go and find Dad, who's in the shed. I remind him that Norman and Mark are coming over.

"We wanted to make CAKES!" I tell him.

"Does it REALLY matter? Mum said it's OK to make BISCUITS."

"I suppose so..."

"Don't worry, Tom. I've got everything under control," Dad tells me. (I'm not so sure.)

I go back to the house just in time for Norman and Mark to arrive. They both brought a few EXTRA ingredients. But no SNAKE.

(Which is a BIG shame.)

173

"They were ALL asleep. I didn't want to disturb them," Mark explains.

(What does he mean THEM? How many snakes has he got?)

Norman's brought a WEIRD-shaped cookie cutter. Which is actually quite useful now that we're making biscuits.

"What is it?" I ask him.

"I think it's a LEAF   or it could be an ALIEN.

It's hard to know," Norman tells me.

Dad comes in from the SHED and says, "RIGHT. Wash your hands, boys, and LET's get started, shall we?"

Dad is trying to be all organized and jolly.

"These biscuits are going to be the BEST EVER," Mark says, while rubbing his tummy and patting his head. Which is NOT easy to do.

We wash our hands, then all have a go at copying Mark. We're just getting the hang of it when the doorbell goes again.

Who's that?

DING

DONG

"Try doing it the other way," Norman tells us.

"I'll get the door," Dad says. "That will be my

SECRET WEAPON."

"What secret weapon?" I ask Dad while patting my head then swapping over hands.

(I'm getting good at this.)

You'll SEE!

"Did someone say BISCUITS?" Granny says, walking in and waving around something that LOOKS like a RECIPE. Which is good NEWS because sometimes Granny's biscuits can be a bit ODD. "I'm here to HELP!" she smiles.

Teeth biscuits

"Just in time! The boys are all ready," Dad tells her — before leaving us to it and going back to his shed.

 "We'll be FINE, won't we, boys?" (I guess so.) "I'm here if you need me," Dad adds.

Granny makes room on the table for all the biscuit ingredients so we can get started.

SHORTBREAD BISCUIT INGREDIENTS

NOT SHORTBREAD BISCUIT INGREDIENTS

Pepper

FLOUR   SUGAR   milk   Butter   SALT

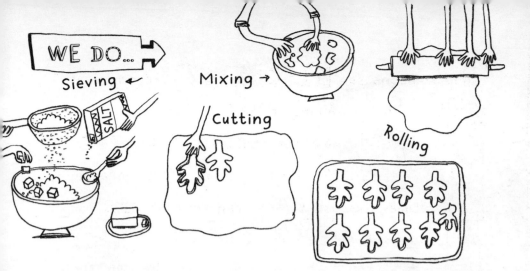

WE DO...

Sieving ←

Mixing →

Cutting

Rolling

Until ... TA DAH! our biscuits are ready to go in the oven.

"Well done, boys. I'll have to bake them in batches as there's SO MANY." (We've made TEN TRAYS!)

We go and watch a cartoon I bought at the charity shop.

"Our biscuits will be EXTRA popular, I think. LET'S EAT SOME NOW!" Norman says, because he's hungry.

"Good thinking. It's important to see what they taste like," I agree.

So when Granny calls us back, that's what we do!

(But there's a problem.)

YUCK!

"EEEEEwwwwwwww..." The biscuits are REVOLTING.

"I don't know what happened," Granny splutters.

"They're really HARD, like ROCKS, and they taste salty," Norman points out. (It's true.)

THIS IS A HUGE DISASTER!

"What are we going to do NOW?" I ask, hoping SOMEONE will have a good idea.

"Can we start again?" Mark wants to know. But I'm not sure there's enough time.

(THIS has happened before ... I'm sure of it.)

Business DAY IS TOMORROW — and Norman and Mark have to go home soon.

Dad comes in from the shed to see how we're getting on.

"Those biscuits *smell* NICE!"

"Try one – you'll change your mind," I warn him.

So he does...

"Oh, dear," Dad says, putting the rest of the biscuit in the bin.

"Can't you just BUY some biscuits?" he suggests.

"NO, Dad. We're supposed to be *MAKING* things to sell. That's the WHOLE POINT!" I explain.

I **look** at Norman and Mark who just shrug their shoulders. Norman tries another biscuit and nearly BREAKS his tooth. CRACK

"It's no good," he winces. "Even I can't eat them."

When Delia comes home she starts causing trouble straight away.

"Help yourself," I mumble in a really FED-UP voice.

Are these biscuits?

"They look a bit ... HARD."

Delia starts TAPPING a biscuit on a plate.

"You're NOT trying to SELL these, are you?"
She's BASHING the biscuit on the table now.
"NOT NOW, we're not. Have you got any good
suggestions?" I say, grumpily, while Norman and
Mark mess around with the biscuits.

Delia goes to the cupboard and brings out
something that looks a bit like BIRD FOOD.

"What's THAT?"

POPCORN.

"Are you SURE?" I ask suspiciously.
"It's not cooked yet, dingbat. You have to POP
it first."

(I knew that.)

"I LOVE popcorn," Norman shouts.
"ME TOO!" Mark adds.

Granny agrees. "What a GREAT IDEA, Delia!"

"Let's use the popcorn maker we gave you last year. It'll be a lot quicker and easier to pop it that way."

I'm **SHOCKED** that Delia has actually been HELPFUL and come up with a GOOD IDEA. (Which is suspiciously nice of her.)

Suspicious

We get started making the popcorn but Granny keeps suggesting ODD FLAVOURS to try.

"How about chilli and orange? That sounds delicious."

(Not to me it doesn't!)

"Kids won't like that, Granny."

"I WOULD!" Norman shouts.

We ignore him and end up making popcorn that is slightly SWEET. And popcorn that is slightly **BLUe**.

"Just a few drops of NATURAL food colouring. See how interesting it looks now?" Granny tells us.

(It just looks BLUE to me.)

Turns out that eating our popcorn makes your hands a bit BLUE - and your teeth too.

"Don't worry. It will wash off," Granny assures us.

She tells Mum exactly the SAME thing...

You're very BLUE.

And Mark's dad (Mr Clump) too when he comes to pick him and Norman up.

Been busy?

While Mark goes to get his COAT, Mum makes me wash my hands in the kitchen. (It turns out Granny is RIGHT after all and it does disappear.)

Mark seems to be taking AGES to come back. "What's he doing?" I wonder and Norman says, "Sounds like he's TALKING to himself."

We can both hear him say,

What are YOU doing here, you naughty snake?

(Did Mark just say SNAKE?)

Yeah!

(He did say SNAKE.)

"Look who I found in my COAT POCKET! He slipped in when I wasn't looking. SNEAKY SNAKE!" Mark shows us his snake, who looks friendly enough. It seems very KEEN to say hello.

Hello!

Mum's not quite so keen – and Delia doesn't stick around at all.

"She's allergic to pets," Mum explains to Mr Clump as Delia disappears upstairs at TOP SPEED. Sadly ☹ Mark's dad makes him put the snake away before he gets too LIVELY.

(I think he means the SNAKE, not Mark.)

Norman is ALWAYS lively and he's waving goodbye.

"See you tomorrow. Mark should bring his SNAKE with him," he shouts.

Mr Clump says that's NOT going to happen.

(Which is a shame.)

But at least I have a TON of NEW ideas to draw in my sketchbook NOW.

Delia coming face-to-face with a snake.

Business DAY is TODAY at last.

(Mum helped bag up the popcorn so it's all ready for me to take to school. It looks pretty good, if I do say so myself.)

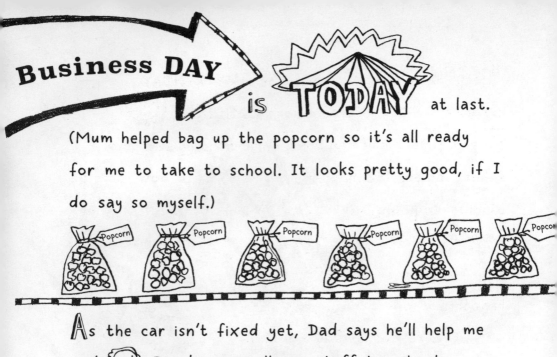

As the car isn't fixed yet, Dad says he'll help me and 😊 Derek carry all our stuff to school (which, in my case, is the bags of popcorn that aren't heavy at all).

"Good luck today!

And, Tom, Granny Mavis and Granddad Bob REALLY want you to GO ROUND and see them after school. I think they have a SURPRISE for you. OK?"

"Yes, Mum," I say. (Not really listening.)

"Let's have BLUE popcorn for my BIRTHDAY surprise, shall we?" Mum says, SMILING.

Every time Mum mentions her birthday Dad and I keep quiet. It's happened a few times now, so Mum's beginning to *THINK* we must be PLANNING some BIG birthday surprise for her. The only surprise so FAR is that we've sold her brooch for one pound.

(We're not telling her THAT.)

"I'm still looking for a brooch, Tom. I'm NOT giving up, BUT, just in case, I have a back-up plan," Dad says to me.

"What's that, Dad?" I wonder.

"Something ... really GREAT."

(Which means he hasn't thought of anything yet. I can tell.)

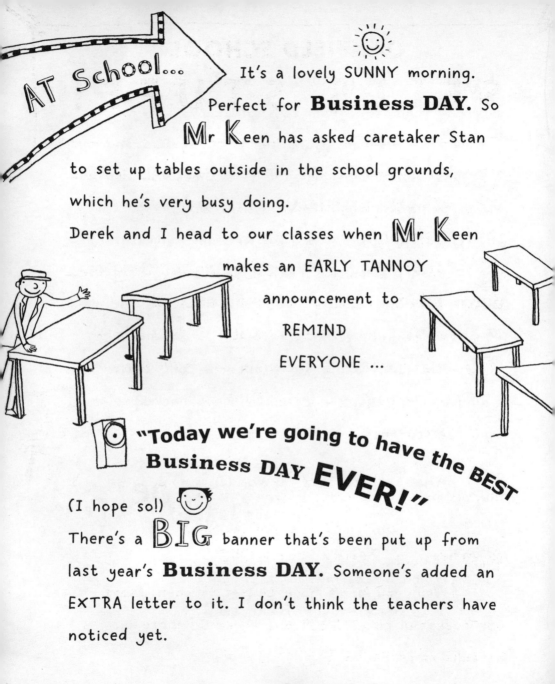

AT School... It's a lovely SUNNY morning. Perfect for **Business DAY.** So **Mr Keen** has asked caretaker Stan to set up tables outside in the school grounds, which he's very busy doing.

Derek and I head to our classes when **Mr Keen** makes an EARLY TANNOY announcement to REMIND EVERYONE ...

"Today we're going to have the BEST Business DAY EVER!"

(I hope so!) There's a **BIG** banner that's been put up from last year's **Business DAY.** Someone's added an EXTRA letter to it. I don't think the teachers have noticed yet.

OAKFIELD SCHOOL
SMELLS STUFF!

Mr Fullerman says we have "NORMAL" lessons until lunchtime and he wants us to carry on with ENGLISH. But nobody can concentrate.

"There's a lot of 'chat' going on. Quieten down, please. I know you're all excited," he says.

Everything that's being SOLD is at the back of the class on tables. Including our POPCORN. I keep turning around to check it's OK.

Marcus says, "Where are your CAKES then?"

"Change of PLAN – we made POPCORN instead."

Marcus pulls a face. "Why's it **BLue?**"

"Why not? It's still yummy."

"It looks YUCK and **WEIRD.**"

"Well, you don't have to eat it then. More for everyone else," I tell him. Then I ignore him as he pulls more FACES.

FINALLY... Mr Fullerman says, **"OK, Class 5F, are you ready to go RIGHT NOW?"**

Then he quickly adds ... **"NO RUNNING!"**

as we all start running out of the door.

Julia and Indrani are both back at school and not sick any more. (Though Julia does keep sniffing. A LOT.) sniff sniff They've helped out by making POSTERS to put up.

"Just CROSS out ~~CAKES~~ and add POPCORN," I suggest when I see what they've done.

Delicious ~~cakes~~ popcorn £1

It doesn't take long to get set up. We find the table with our names on it. (Which helps.)

Tom Mark Norman

Julia Indrani

I notice all the food stalls are grouped together. We're next to the FRUIT KEBABS. Which is EXCELLENT news and not much competition for us. (Popcorn or fruit kebabs is an easy choice.)

Mrs Mumble  comes around and gives us all a small amount of CHANGE in a box. "It's called a 'FLOAT' and it's not for you to SPEND! Now you'll have change to give to people."

"Imagine how many caramel wafers we could buy with that," Norman says.

"YUM!" (I'm imagining LOADS.)

"We're not allowed," Julia tells us,

as if we would...

(Shame, though.)

I've got two pounds to spend on something. I haven't decided on WHAT (yet). We're all ready to go when the BELL rings and kids come streaming out of their classrooms.

So far it's all going WELL. Our blue popcorn seems popular.

CAKES POPCORN HERE!   CAKES POPCORN HERE!

Then Marcus appears wearing his SUPERHERO costume and holding a sign. He stands right in front of our popcorn, so I say, "Hey, Marcus, is that working then?" and he says, "Of course it's working – EVERYONE is looking at me."

(Like I should be impressed.)

"I meant your sign, not your costume," I point out.

"Well, we've sold LOADS of comic folders and my sign is pointing them in the right direction. You've got a lot of BLUE popcorn still. I'm not surprised," he says smugly. But BEFORE I can answer, a group of kids ask him, "Are you selling popcorn?"

HEY!

COMIC FOLDERS

Popcorn

"No, I'm not," he tells them grumpily. So they ⟨RUSH past him to get to OUR table.

"Sorry, Marcus. I can't talk now. I'm too busy selling our BLUE popcorn." (Which is true.)

Yum

See, loads of kids are buying it.

It's not long before we only have
TWO PACKETS LEFT.

"Let's SHARE them!" Norman suggests, which is
an EXCELLENT idea. So that's what we do.

(We're only checking it tastes OK ...

which it does.)

ALL GONE

Mrs Mumble sees that we're all finished and comes
over to collect our money. She's impressed that
we've sold everything.

Good job. Well done!

We've got some time to look around ourselves now.
So I *rush* straight over to see Derek because
I want a go at the Treasure Hunt. It takes me a
LONG TIME to decide WHERE to put my TWO FLAGS
and Derek is not much help at all.

Yes!   No.
       Maybe...

Hurry up, Tom!
Anywhere will do...

I hope I win!

I have **ONE POUND** left to spend and I REALLY want to BUY a treat. ☺ Something tasty. (Not a fruit kebab, though. I LIKE fruit – but I want something a LOT more TREAT-like.)

The cakes I've seen look tempting 🧁🧁🧁 but then I 😊 ⌐ ⌐ ⌐ SPOT these interesting, tasty-looking, crispy crunchy bar things. ▰

Lots of kids are eating them so they must be NICE.

But while I am (thinking) 😟 about what I should buy (cake? Crunchy bar thing? Cake?) Mrs Mumble BLOWS a whistle and says,

FIVE MINUTES LEFT, EVERYBODY, THEN IT'S BACK TO CLASS! FIVE MINUTES!

Which makes me PANIC as I haven't made up my mind YET. 😟 Then loads of kids _swoop_ down on the CAKES like **VULTURES** and

before I can CHOOSE

they're all `\\'''''` GONE! `''''`

↑(Empty plates)

No way! I shout, but it's too late. So I turn around and head as quickly as I can towards the LAST FEW crispy crunchy bars. I can SEE that there are only THREE LEFT.

Now there are only TWO... QUICK... QUICK... ONE LEFT.

I shout at the kid nearest the table, "I'LL TAKE THAT, IT'S MINE!"

Thankfully, Brad Galloway hears me and says, "Hi, Tom. You're LUCKY, it's the last one."

Then he puts it in a bag for me. Which is a BIG RELIEF. I'm in such a hurry to hand over my pound that it kind of FLICKS out of my hand ...

... and as Brad goes to catch it he lets go of the bag ...

... which drops to the floor like a stone. BUT the crispy crunchy bar is fine and safe inside the bag. (which is lucky!)

Then someone accidentally TREADS on it – and it's not fine any more.

"Sorry, Tom. You could buy something else? There's still time," Brad suggests and hands back my pound.

"Maybe..." I sigh, looking at the crispy crunchy crumbs.

Whoops!

Squashed bar.

Back in class Marcus asks,

"WHAT'S THAT?"

"A fruit Kebab. I like fruit Kebabs."

(It's better than nothing.)

"Is that ALL you bought?" he adds.

"No, I've entered the Treasure Hunt as well."

"Me too," Marcus says, then he starts going ON

about how brilliant HIS group was to sell ALL their

AMAZING comic folders.

(Yawn...)

Mr Fullerman congratulates EVERYONE for

working so hard on **Business DAY.**

**"Mr Keen will announce the winner
of the Treasure Hunt at the end of the
school day."**

"I can't wait," I whisper.

"Tom, hurry up and STOP eating," he tells me. **"And, Marcus, take off your cape and mask."**

With the last bit of fruit eaten, I resist the temptation to fiddle with the wooden stick since Mr Fullerman is still watching me. When Marcus takes off his mask I pretend to be SHOCKED by his REAL face.

It's hideous!

"Ha ha – very funny, Tom," he says.

(It is quite funny.) That's when I notice something else that's funny about him.

"Did you eat any popcorn, Marcus?"

"No, I told you it looked yucky. Who wants blue popcorn?"

But I'm not sure he's telling the truth.

Close-up teeth

(Blue popcorn + Marcus = blue teeth.)

Before the end of school, Mr Keen announces the **WINNER** of the Treasure Hunt. And the BAD NEWS is

it's not me.

(Awwww.)

It's not difficult to SPOT the person who did win.

YES!

It's Solid, who jumps up and does a LAP of honour around the **WHOLE** class while CHEERING. **THE GOOD NEWs** is Solid says he's going to share some of his treasure

TREATS with his friends. Which is REALLY nice of him and **not** something many kids would do (mentioning no names).

When the bell goes **OFF** for the end of school,

Solid can't **WAIT** to go and collect his

* **TREASURE** * TREATS.  Pens Choc coins Yes!

I'm about to follow him out when **AMY** asks me,

"Are you coming to the

park after school, Tom?

There's a group of us going and some parents too.

Solid is coming."

Solid + Treasure + Park = Choc treats.

BRILLIANT

"Count me **IN**," I say. "I can call my dad and

tell him where we're going."

This is shaping up to be a **REALLY**

FUN DAY. **AMY** says to meet them by

the school gate.

But when I go outside ...

THE FOSSILS

ARE WAITING FOR ME.

(Which is a surprise.)

Then I remember I was

SUPPOSED to be going to

see them after school.

(At least Granddad's [not] holding his teeth in his

HAND.)

I run over to see them and Granny says,

"How did your popcorn sell then?"

"FANTASTIC. We sold it ALL!" I tell her.

"Well done, Tom. We thought we'd save you

the trouble of walking over and come to meet you."

"I can see!"

"Now let's get going because we have

a SURPRISE for you," says Granddad.

Which sounds interesting.

Solid walks past holding his PRIZE.

"See you at the PARK, Tom!" he says, looking

happy. Then Marcus (who's behind him) adds,

"There'll be more treats for us if you're not

coming – just saying." (Thanks for that, Marcus.)

"We can come to the park with you and leave

the surprise for ANOTHER day if you want, Tom?"

"But it MIGHT not be there tomorrow," Granddad says.

(Now I don't know what to do.)

IT'S SO TRICKY making up my mind sometimes ...
LIKE **NOW**.

PARK? ➡ YES!

SKIP the surprise? ➡ NO.

Ask Solid to
save me a treat? ➡ (Maybe...)

(THE FOSSILS are still waiting.) So I say,

"The park can wait, Granny and Granddad."

"Lovely! Let's go ..." Granny smiles, and then adds,

... SHOPPING!

(Which is **NOT** what I was expecting to do.)

"Oh... Shopping. Great, I can't wait," I say.

I'm already regretting my decision NOT to go

to the park with my friends to eat treats. (Sigh.)

THE FOSSILS KEEP stopping to LOOK at

stuff I'd NEVER normally LOOK at.

Candles
cushions
Fluffy slippers

I TRY not to get bored and keep occupied by

SPOTTING kids who have **BLue** TEETH

from eating our popcorn. There's quite a few

Hi, Tom

There's one →

walking home. Granddad tells us that if

HIS teeth went BLUE, he'd take

them out ...

"And give them a GOOD scrub," he laughs. I think my teeth might still be a bit blue, but I can't see.

"We're NEARLY there, Tom," Granny says, which is just as well because Granddad has his stick and is quite slow at walking. We turn the corner and STOP right outside the same CHARITY SHOP we took the VASE and MUGS to, AND my MINI DRUM KIT as well. (Great. I've missed the park and fun to come to the CHARITY SHOP - AGAIN.)

"Let's go in, shall we?" Granddad says. I make the BEST of the situation and try to find the kid's section. They have books and films that might be interesting. Then Granddad POINTS to something and says,

"Is that any good for you, Tom?"

I turn round and see ...

... WHAT **LOOKS** like a BRAND-NEW

MINI SCOOTER!

"I really wanted one of **THOSE!**"

"Let's get it for you then," Granny tells me.

I give them both a hug and say,

"THANK YOU!"

(I KNEW I did the right thing

coming with **THE FOSSILS** !)

I pick up the scooter and take it to the till, where

the lady looks at the label and says,

"That's TEN POUNDS, please. It's BRAND NEW."

Then something goes **PING** in my brain.

I'm sure I've heard her voice before.

I look up and I can't believe who it is...

THE OLD LADY who bought Mum's brooch from the BOOT SALE (without her scarf).

I have to ask her about the brooch, but she says,

"The scooter's TEN POUNDS," again because I am just  STARING at her. Then as Granddad is about to pay, I look down and THERE IS

MUM'S CAT BROOCH

in the glass cabinet.

I'm so EXCITED to find it I want to shout,

YES! I've FOUND IT!

But then I realize I'll have to BUY it.
I look at the price tag and it says TEN pounds.
WHAT? I don't have enough money (or ANY money).
I quickly ask Granddad,

"WAIT! Can I get something ELSE too?"

Which sounds a BiT GREEDY. **So** I try and explain.

"It's not for ME. It's a PRESENT for Mum's birthday. She'd LOVE that brooch!" Granny and Granddad look a bit SURPRISED.

"Are you SURE? It's quite a LOT for a funny-looking CAT brooch."

"Mum collects them – I KNOW she'd be SO HAPPY to get this one. I wouldn't ask you, but this would be the best present EVER!"

There's a big sign that says CASH ONLY. Granddad checks his wallet. "I don't have enough – I'll have to go to the cash machine."

I tell them, "I'd rather get the BROOCH than the scooter." (Just trying to be helpful.)

Granddad says, "That's OK – we'll get both."

"You must REALLY want the brooch, Tom," Granny says.

(YES, I DO. They have NO idea!)

Granddad walks off (VERY slowly) to get some more money – which isn't far.

I'm keeping an EYE 👁 on the CAT brooch 🐱 to make sure no one else NABS it, when the old lady says, "*Didn't I see you at ... where was it? The boot sale, that's right!*"

I don't want Granny to find out that we SOLD Mum's brooch for one pound and are buying it BACK, so I say quietly, "No, it wasn't me ... not me at all."

"*Are you <u>sure</u>? I bought something from you. <u>What</u> was it now? It'll come back to me.*"

(Uh-oh.) I pretend that I can't hear what she's saying and quickly walk off to l⊙⊙k at some OLD records (that will do). Fingers crossed she won't remember. I'm LOOKING through the records and there's loads of bands I recognize from Mr Fingle's collection. Then I come across something...

NOT ONE, but TWO **PLASTIC CUP** albums.

WOO HOO!

THIS is TURNING OUT TO BE MY LUCKY DAY!

(I LOVE CHARITY SHOPS ... NOW.)

Derek told me **PLASTIC CUP** albums are worth LOADS of money. I should DEFINITELY get them BOTH - but as I don't have any money I'm going to have to ask  again.

Granddad comes back into the shop (slowly) holding another ten-pound note.

"Here we go, Tom. Let's get your scooter AND that funny-looking brooch for your mum."

"Can I get these as well?" I ask, holding up the records.

THE FOSSILS give me a LOOK and SIGH REALLY loudly. They don't say "NO", but I get the HINT.

(I'll get them another time.)

While the old lady is wrapping up the brooch (which HASN'T jogged her memory YET), I keep looking at the ground with my hands in my pockets, trying not to make EYE CONTACT with her.

I can feel something a bit like paper squished up right at the bottom of my pocket.

I take it out and unfold what TURNS out to be a MASHED UP TEN-POUND NOTE! It's the one Dad gave me at the boot sale! (I'd forgotten about it!) BRILLIANT!

"HEY, LOOK WHAT I'VE FOUND!" I shout, and I wave my slightly manky money around. I am SO HAPPY because now I can get the mini scooter, Mum's brooch AND two PLASTIC CUP albums (that only cost one pound each). I give THE FOSSILS FIVE pounds back to pay for (most of) the brooch and keep THREE to buy CARAMEL WAFERS on the way home. (RESULT.)

211

I don't bother going to the park now because I can't WAIT to get home and tell Dad what's happened.  Yes! (And Derek too.)

Granny and Granddad walk back with me (S L O W L Y). But they don't come in because Granny says, "We won't stop. I'm cooking dinner for some old friends tonight."

Granddad holds up the wafer I gave him.

"Don't panic - I have my EMERGENCY wafer just in case."

Which makes me laugh. Ha! Ha!

"I don't mind if you want to cook," Granny tells him.

"Better go, Tom, or I'll be in trouble," Granddad whispers.

I HUG them BOTH, take my scooter, albums and the brooch, then go and find Dad.

He's in his shed, working. Yum...

I COULD tell him straight away. Or I could have

some FUN. (What to do?)

(That's EASY, really...)

Brooch behind my back

"Guess what Granny and Granddad got

from the CHARITY SHOP for me?"

I ask Dad first.

"Hi, Tom - was it a mini scooter?"

"YES! HOW DID YOU KNOW?"

"Just a hunch."

"OK, what else did I get then?"

"You got more? An old vase?"

"NO - try again."

"Another GUITAR?"

"I WISH - keep guessing."

"Hmmm ... a spaceship?"

"Now you're being silly - give up?"

Dad nods - so I SHOW him the brooch.

"YES, TOM!"

He cheers and *SWINGS* me around.

Which is tricky to do in a small shed.

 "You are the CLEVEREST boy in the WHOLE WORLD."

I AGREE. (Thank you, thank you.)

Dad has a look at the brooch, which seems

to be fine (though the eyes are still wonky).

We're so BUSY celebrating that neither of

us spot MUM, who's standing at the door and

LOOKING at us.

 "You two are very happy. What's the GOOD NEWS?"

"NOTHING!"

we both say.

Dad hides the brooch in his hand. "People with a birthday coming up shouldn't ask questions," Dad tells her.

"EXACTLY," I say. (Good thinking, Dad.)

"OK, OK..." Mum says and goes back into the house. I'd forgotten about getting Mum a present from ME. I could give her my cuckoo clock.

I'm not sure.

Maybe I will ... maybe I won't.

(I haven't decided yet.)

With Mum SAFELY back in the house, Dad takes out the brooch. "I'll get the EYES fixed and put it in a fancy box for her birthday," he tells me. It's a good plan.

"I'm SO pleased we got it back," Dad says.

Me too! (PHEW!)

This seems like a GOOD time to get out my SKETCHBOOK.

It's getting pretty FULL because over the last few days there's been a LOT going on.

I've drawn as many things as I can REMEMBER and written a few NOTES to help explain what's going on in the pictures, in case Mr Fullerman gets confused when he sees it.

(It happens.)

Mr Fullerman being confused

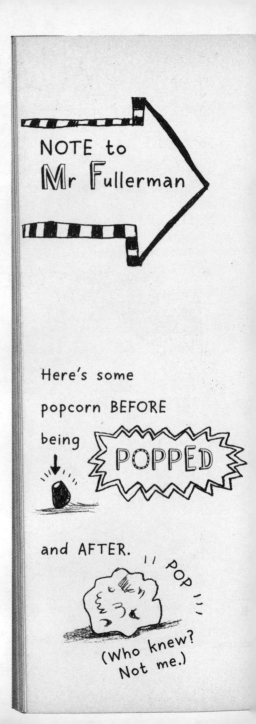

NOTE to Mr Fullerman

Here's some popcorn BEFORE being POPPED

and AFTER.

POP

(Who knew? Not me.)

I don't have a **BLue** pen, so you'll have to IMAGINE that THIS  is BLUE.

(My hair's not blue though.)

This is ME being VERY HAPPY because the popcorn we made for **Business DAY** sold REALLY WELL.

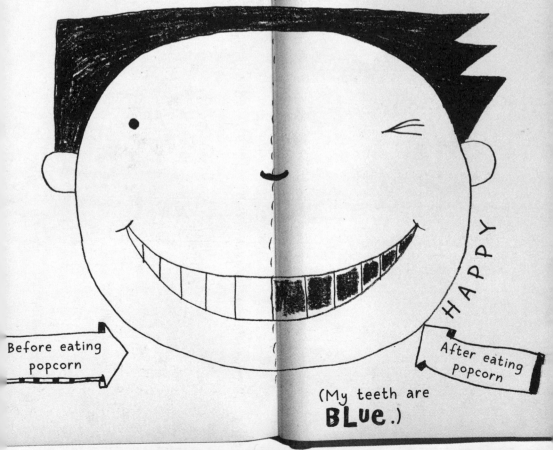

Before eating popcorn

HAPPY

After eating popcorn

(My teeth are **BLue**.)

My dad

Ceiling

YES!

World-record jump

Here's Dad looking happier than I've seen him for a **LONG** time because of something I **FOUND**. (I can't say what it was in case my mum sees this. But it was good.)

Here's what Marcus would look like if he turned slowly into a troll.

This is showing a wide VARIETY of facial expressions (in case you're wondering WHY I'm drawing this).

YUCK

CLOSE-UP of TROLL hair and head

(I'll do more later.)

The next day

I SPY

I'm minding my own business when I notice that Delia has accidentally left her KEY in the door. I can't hear her, so it seems like a good idea to see WHAT she's been up to. I'm just about to take a L⊙⊙K when Mum says,

"What are you doing going into Delia's room, Tom?"

Huh?

So I blurt out, "Delia's left the KEY in her door. SEE!" Which gets Mum's attention.

"Don't touch it. I'll get your dad. He can go and see what's going on. Just in case."

(I'm thinking - just in case of WHAT? Delia really is an alien after all? I have my suspicions.)

Don't come in.

While Mum's getting Dad, I try looking through the keyhole. But I can't see very much – it's just DARK.  "Don't be nosy, Tom," Mum tells me as she catches me again. "Off you go back to your room. And don't <u>you</u> tell your sister we found her key. We'll do that if we need to. OK?"

I say, "OK". (This could be good information to use with Delia at a later date.)

I'm in my room, but still PEERING round the door.

I can't see much as they're STANDING IN THE WAY. Which is annoying.

Turns OUT I'm not the ONLY ONE in this
family who LIKES drawing and doodling (sort of).
I can hear Mum and Dad say,

SHOCKED FACES

Delia's been PAINTING?

"Gosh, I wasn't expecting to find all these
BIG paintings in here," Mum says to Dad.

(Paintings?)

"I wonder why she didn't tell us," Dad says.

"Can I SEE?" I shout from my room. Mum
and Dad ignore me and carry on chatting.

"Maybe she's planning on showing them to us later."

Before I can SNEAK behind them to take a look at Delia's "PAINTINGS", Mum and Dad have already LOCKED the door again.

"Awww, I want to SEE Delia's **weird** paintings!" I say, trying to persuade them.

"You don't need to see or SAY anything about her paintings. And they aren't **weird.**"

"They are a bit ... WILD," Dad says.

"She's just expressing herself," Mum explains.

"Because she's **weird.**" I add. Mum and Dad give me a LOOK. Before they start asking me if I have any HOMEWORK to do - which usually happens when I'm in trouble - I go back to my room.

MAYBE Delia and I have more in common than I thought. We BOTH LOVE **DUDES** ☑ and drawing ☑ and painting ☑, even though I haven't seen them yet. Speaking of which...

Here's a DOODLE I did drawing around my hand and half a biscuit. It took me a while to do – but the biscuit kept me going.

Keeping my PROMISE to Mum and Dad about not telling Delia how they'd snuck into her room and seen her **weird** paintings is a LOT trickier than I expected. ESPECIALLY when I discovered what she'd done to <u>MY</u> cuckoo clock. I heard some VERY ODD noises coming from my room and found THIS IN MY BIN!

OOOK oOOWW
OOOOoOOK ooWOoWW
OOOK oOOWW

Delia had taped up the clock door so the cuckoo just kept bashing its head on it...

Admittedly my cuckoo clock HAS been going off at RANDOM times. But I LIKE the noise it makes.

CucKoo

I CHARGED down to Delia's room and stood outside SHOUTING,

"STAY OUT OF MY ROOM and DON'T touch my **CucKoo** clock again, OR ELSE!"

(I wanted to say, "Or else I'll put TAPE all over your **weird** PAINTINGS!" But I didn't.)

I <u>knew</u> Delia was there because I could SMELL the paint. But she just kept quiet.

Now I know my clock drives her **MAD.** I'm going to KEEP it and set it as often as possible. Ha!

I don't have a present for Mum's birthday now but it's **AGES** away. When is it again? Oh, I remember now...

It's TOMORROW.

No problem, I'll make her a **COMIC** folder

As Mum **GAVE** away most of my comics it
will have to be small. (I'll remind her about that.)
I go back to my room and get out the few comics
I have left. I'm all set to make Mum's present.
Right after I've read the comics again...

CucKooo
CucKoooo
CucKooooo

Mum's Birthday Surprise

The breakfast in bed I made for Mum didn't go EXACTLY to plan. (How was I supposed to know there was a SPIDER in the FLOWERS I picked from the garden?) The spider made Mum jump out of bed. The TOAST survived but the orange juice and cereal. SPILT EVERYWHERE!

After Mum got over the SHOCK (and cleaned up the mess) she said it was a LOVELY thought and VERY kind of me. ☺

Favourite child.

(Mum didn't say that, but I'm sure I am.)

Mum <u>did</u> say she was going shopping with some of her friends today. Dad did a good job of pretending to be SAD ☹ about not being able to go with her.

"What a SHAME I have to cook and get ready for your special birthday dinner tonight."

Dad <u>IS</u> HAPPY ☺ about me finding that cat brooch though. He's managed to have its EYES fixed as part of Mum's present. I can't WAIT to see her FACE when she opens the box! There's MORE GOOD NEWS, because Dad's asked Derek and his mum and dad to come round as well.

Mum's gone and invited the cousins, Aunty Alice and Uncle Kevin too. She says, "I couldn't NOT ask them."

"Great – I love it when Uncle Kevin comments on my food," Dad tells her.

"He might NOT," Mum says.

(He definitely WILL.)

229

What's that?

Derek comes round EARLY and brings ROOSTER, which is a good opportunity to see how his TRICKS are coming along.

Rooster, DANCE!

I tell Derek that I'm IMPRESSED.
"He's learnt to POINT too."

"I can see." Rooster is one smart dog. We spend the next ten minutes getting Rooster to point at things.

Rooster, POINT!

Granny and Granddad arrive with Mum's CAKE, which still needs decorating. "I thought you'd like to help me," Granny tells Derek and me.

"I've bought LARGE white ⚪ chocolate buttons and small milk ⚫ chocolate buttons to cover the cake," she explains, which helps us to make up our minds about helping. Mmmmmmm

"YES, we'll help!" I tell Granny.

(Last year Granny decorated the cake with bread sticks, so chocolate buttons are a BIG improvement.)

Granny shows us how she'd like it done. We have to stick the milk choc button on to the white choc button with a blob of icing. ⚫ "Don't eat them!" Granny tells us.

rooster pointing

(Too late...)

It's only when we've finished that we notice the cake LOOKS like it's covered in EYES. →

I go and get my present and put it next to the EYE CAKE. Delia appears out of her room and says, "That cake looks CREEPY."
So I tell her she doesn't have to EAT it.

"More for us – and Mum." (It is her cake, I suppose.) Then I ask her WHERE her present for Mum is. "Did you forget?" I wonder.

"I'll bring it down later – and STOP putting that STUPID CUCKOO CLOCK so close to my WALL," she tells me slightly crossly.

(Ha! It's working then!)

I tell Derek about my TWO **PLASTIC CUP** albums and HE thinks his dad will want to buy at least ONE of them from me. Which would be GREAT because then I could buy all kinds of good stuff. Derek says, "The album he's got is a bit scratched. Don't worry, he doesn't know it was us."

(PHEW!)

Catch

"Dad thinks Rooster did it when he jumped up and made the needle skid over the album – I said nothing!"

SCRAPE

"That's lucky!" I agree.

While we're waiting for Mum to come home from shopping and everyone else to arrive, I tell Derek all about the CAT BROOCH.

Like this – Wow

Then we try and sneak a peak at Delia's paintings, but her door's locked.

"Let's have a spacehopper race instead!" I suggest, which Derek thinks is an EXCELLENT idea. I HOPE Mum's birthday surprise will BE JUST AS MUCH FUN.

(GUESS WHAT?
Turns out ... it WAS!)

Even Uncle Kevin didn't manage to spoil it for Dad,
who managed to **WIN** his spacehopper race after a
s l o w start. Mum said the way Dad PUNCHED
the air and kept saying, "YES! YES! YES!"

was a bit over the top. I just thought it was
FUNNY. ☺

Me and Derek took as many chocolate eyes off
the cake as we could get away with.

I ate most of them but started to feel
slightly sick, so I SAVED some for later.

LATER = NOW

(I did these doodles before finishing off my
sketchbook ... and the buttons.)

YUM!

Ha!
Ha!

HELLO

Note for
Mr Fullerman.
Please
read.

Sorry about the EXTRA paper I've stuck into my book. I just couldn't FIT all the drawings on to the last few pages.

I had to ADD MORE!

My mum's birthday surprise was a bit more eventful than I expected. There was a LOT to draw. I've written some VERY helpful comments next to the pictures, which I HOPE WILL EXPLAIN STUFF.

And, as you're feeling much better now,
I'm hoping you might say,

WOW, Tom GATES has done REALLY
well here. I think he deserves more
merits than ANYONE else.

(Just saying...)

(No pressure, sir...)

At **Mum's BIRTHDAY SURPRISE** there were some VERY GOOD EXPRESSIONS to draw. HERE ARE JUST A FEW.

Burning smell
Burning smell

(Not-so-good cooking.)

Dad when Mum turns up with EMERGENCY FOOD.

Phew.

BIN

Dad cooking (confidently) - Not for long - Mum saves the day.

Note for Mr Fullerman

Derek embarrassed by his dad's T-shirt.

PLASTIC CUP

PLASTIC CUP is a BAND from ancient times, in case you didn't know.

Pretend Surprise

Lovely, Delia.

That's great!

Delia's painting

Mum (and Dad) pretending they'd NEVER seen the painting that Delia gave Mum for her birthday.

My sister Delia

Delia looking EXACTLY the same as she always does.

Delia said the painting was ABSTRACT. I whispered to Derek to ask if that was another word for "WEIRD". We couldn't work out what it was.

> My cousins after I told them they'd just eaten a bowl of VEGETABLE crisps.
>
> That's a parsnip you're eating.

My cousins - eating

Best of all, here's **MUM** when Dad gave her his birthday present. (The CAT BROOCH with the FIXED EYES and a voucher for some NEW 👠 SHOES.)

> THANK YOU SO **MUCH!**

(Mum [not] just pretending to be happy ...

but actually happy.)

My mum's very old cat brooch.

Before fixing | After fixing

Note for Mr Fullerman This brooch belonged to
a very old person in my mum's family
(a great-great granny). She gave it to my mum. It
wouldn't be my idea of a present, but Dad got the
EYES fixed to be slightly LESS wonky and Mum's
pleased. So is Dad.

Phew.

(I can't say WHY Dad is
so pleased in case Mum
reads this. If she is reading
this – it was nothing!
Honestly...)

Derek doing stupid things with chocolate-button-cake EYES. (I picked some off to eat later.)

Derek's dad when I show him one of the **Plastic Cup** albums I have.

He wants to buy it.

June <u>not</u> laughing

No scratches

Rooster jumping, pointing and dancing (at the same time).

I thought Rooster was the BEST part of Mum's birthday celebration. **UNTIL** we got the spacehoppers out and had RACES. 😊

Dad and Uncle Kevin
racing around the
garden.

Here are some
FACIAL EXPRESSIONS
of other people jumping
on the spacehoppers.

Derek

June

Ponytail

June's dad

Mum

EVEN Delia had a go.

(I added the

FLIES ... ha!)

If you're wondering what Delia's painting

LOOKED LIKE, I tried to recreate it with

some PAINT. ⟹

Delia's painting (by Me).

It got a bit messy. But it looked a bit like THAT.

I hope you like my sketchbook.

Tom,

Thanks for adding the extra paper.

What an excellent sketchbook full
of really interesting faces and
expressions!

I think you have earnt quite a
few merits for all the work
you've put in.

Well done!

But just one thing. I still haven't
had your fairy tale written work!

You could get even more merits if
you hand that in as well.

Mr Fullerman

(And just for your information I do
remember Plastic Cup. They were a
great band.)

GOOD NEWS!

Mr Fullerman says I'm going to get LOADS OF MERITS, which I'm pleased about. ☺

AND he compliments me in front of the WHOLE class as well, which shuts Marcus up because he KEEPS ON telling me how I missed out on all the ☆FUN☆ and `TREATS` by not coming to the park.

Then AMY says, "He's EXAGGERATING. No one stayed for that long, anyway."

So I tell them both about how I found my mum's brooch AND the TWO PLASTIC CUP albums that are worth LOADS of money. AMY's impressed.

Wow! Marcus pretends not to be. Whatever.

Then he asks to have a LOOK in my SKETCHBOOK because I've left it on the desk. For a change I let him. He flicks through it and says,

"It's not bad, Tom. But can you STOP drawing me as a TROLL – it's annoying."

"OK, Marcus, I will," I say.

MY FAIRY TALE homework

The Annoying Little Troll

By Tom Gates

Once upon a time there was a small troll who was a real know-it-all. The other trolls were fed up with listening to him going ON and ON about how he was the smartest troll in the WORLD. He used to PINCH the other trolls' ideas and pretend they were HIS.

This comic folder is MY idea.

One day the annoying little troll thought he would play a trick on everyone. So he SHOUTED,

QUICK! QUICK! There's a BIG monster coming over the hill to EAT ME UP! SAVE ME! HELP!

ALL the Trolls ⏤RAN to his rescue. But when they saw it was a TRICK, they weren't best pleased.

Ha! Ha! Ha! Ha!

"You lot are SO stupid – there's NO MONSTER!" he told them.

The other trolls thought he was hilarious.

(NOT.)

Then one day a BIG HUNGRY MONSTER really did turn up. The trolls could see it creeping up behind the annoying troll and they tried to WARN him (because they were nice trolls).

RUN, RUN! There's a BIG monster behind you who's going to EAT you UP! We can SEE IT. LEG IT quickly!"

The little (annoying) troll said,

"I'm not falling for that OLD trick.

Do you think I'm STUPID?

I might be small – but I'm VERY..."

said the monster as
he popped the annoying little troll into his mouth.

THE END.

YES!
NO.
(Maybe...)

I've finished my fairy tale homework and I'm flicking through the TV channels (as you do) and trying to decide WHAT to watch, when I suddenly come across one of Mum's favourite programmes.

(It's ANTIQUE TREASURES.) I'm about to flick over when SUDDENLY something catches my EYE. There's a man talking about a brooch that looks a bit like Mum's CAT brooch.

Is it?

Maybe... I keep watching, and it does look like her brooch.

The EXPERT is holding it in his hand. So I LISTEN to what he's saying.

This is a VERY rare example of a
CAT BROOCH made by the renowned jeweller
Froubergé.

It looks like the cat's EYES are wonky, but that's
the way the brooch was made. The design was
based on Froubergé's OWN cat, whose
eyes were crossed.

I'm DELIGHTED to see THIS cat's EYES are
still nicely crossed and haven't been mistakenly
"FIXED" or straightened, which makes this
brooch a really collectible item.
A cat brooch with straightened EYES is a LOT
less valuable.

So congratulations to you!

uh-oh...

How hard can it be to make the cat's eyes go WONKY again?

I'd better go and tell Dad...

How to Make a Comic Folder

You will need:
THREE pages of a comic to make a big folder

Ribbon or string

Enough sticky-back plastic to cover all three pages front and back

Some scissors

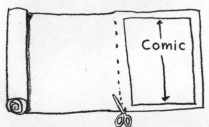

Comic

Peel back the paper from the S.B.P.

Cut <u>SIX</u> pieces of sticky-back plastic – slightly larger than your comic pages (S.B.P. = sticky back plastic).

Get an adult to help you for this bit as S.B.P. can be tricky! Make sure you have a clean surface too. (No biscuit crumbs!)

Comic — Sticky side up

Carefully place your comic page on top of the S.B.P. Start at one end and GENTLY rub the comic as you go.

Repeat with <u>ALL</u> three pages.

Then trim the corners OFF like this. ➡

Turn the comic over and fold down the edges.

Comic

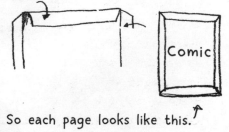

Comic

So each page looks like this. ↑

Then do the same thing with the <u>other</u> side of the comic page.

Comic | Comic front

Choose which page you want for the front. Then cut a strip of S.B.P. and stick two pages together. Trim off the edges <u>or</u> fold them over.

You should have THREE fully covered pages at the end.
Now it's time to stick them together.

To make the pocket <u>inside,</u> fold the last page in half.

Place on the inside right (folded EDGE up).

Folded edge

Then cut <u>MORE</u> strips of S.B.P. to stick the pocket in place.

Comic folder <u>INSIDE</u> | Open pocket

Fold over S.B.P. to make it look neater and stick the pocket in place. It should look like THIS.

Should <u>fit</u> a piece of paper.

To finish off, close the folder and PUNCH a hole in the middle. Then thread your ribbon or string through to HOLD it together.

ONE COMIC FOLDER!

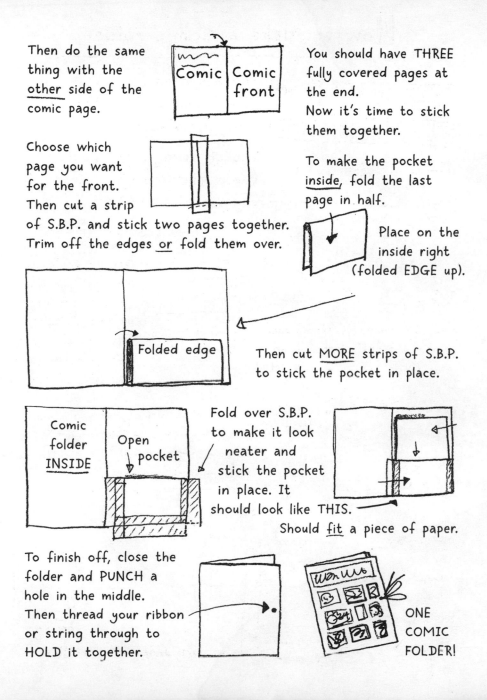

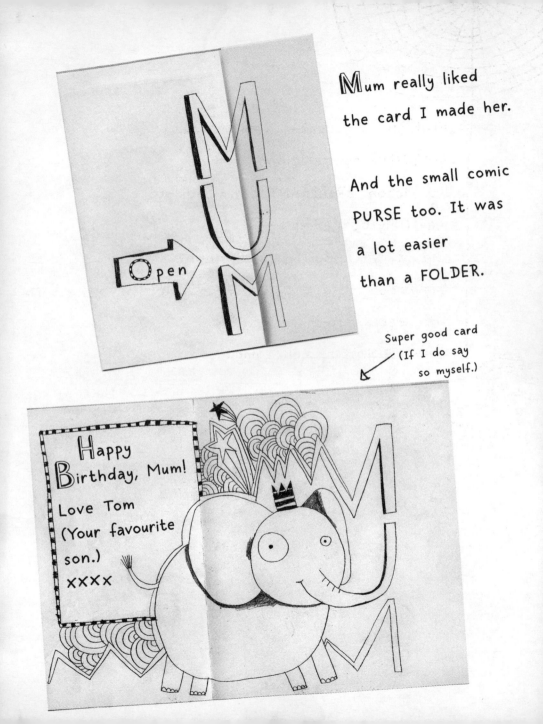

Mum really liked the card I made her.

And the small comic PURSE too. It was a lot easier than a FOLDER.

Super good card (If I do say so myself.)

Happy Birthday, Mum!

Love Tom (Your favourite son.)
xxxx

Visit the Tom Gates website for
AMAZING competitions, to meet
Liz Pichon, BRILLIANT downloads, to
play GENIUS games and to sign up to
the EXTRA SPECIAL newsletter to be
the FIRST to get all the EXCELLENT
Tom Gates news!
www.scholastic.co.uk/tomgatesworld

When Liz ◯ was little Ω, she loved to draw, paint and make things. Her mum used to say she was very good at making a mess (which is still true today!).

She kept drawing and went to art school, where she earned a degree in graphic design. She worked as a designer and art director in the music industry 🎸, and her freelance work has appeared on a wide variety of products.

Liz is the author-illustrator of several picture books. Tom Gates is the first series of books she has written and illustrated for older children. They have won several prestigious awards ⭐, including the Roald Dahl Funny Prize, the Waterstones Children's Book Prize, and the Blue Peter Book Award. The books have been translated into thirty-six languages worldwide.

Visit her at www.LizPichon.com

Rooster's NEW dance moves
(skills)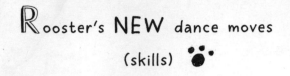